Sex, mystery, and adventure follow Tessa and Ana as they try to protect the revolutionary plastic that Ana's boyfriend, Hans the toymaker, has built into Ana's dolls.

Wealthy plastics entrepreneur Alex Baxter offers to help — but it's Alex's evil partner who has trapped Hans in the company's research centre at the top of the Jungfraujoch mountain. Is Alex friend or enemy? Can Tessa trust him — and can they reach Hans and protect the formula in time?

A Love Of Dolls
Copyright © 2023 Pippa Newnton
ISBN: 978-1-4874-3741-1
Cover art by Tyffani Lyons

Published by eXtasy Books Inc

Look for us online at:
www.eXtasybooks.com

A Love Of Dolls

By

Pippa Newnton

DEDICATION

For Frances

CHAPTER ONE

How could he do this to me? Her anger still boiled inside. Tessa shrugged her hair back from her eyes and tried to concentrate on the conference brochure in front of her, but it was no good. Rob's treachery wouldn't leave her mind.

I thought we were in a loving, caring, relationship, and instead he cheated on me. She turned the page angrily. The smell of hot coffee interrupted her thoughts as an air stewardess came rattling along with a trolley.

She stopped at Tessa's seat. "Coffee and a sandwich?"

Tessa looked up. "No thank you, just coffee."

As the stewardess poured her coffee and handed it to her, the man in the seat beside her looked up from the papers he had been studying.

"What sandwiches do you have?" he asked.

"We have egg and cress, or cheese." The stewardess glanced down at the trolley.

"Are you sure you don't want a sandwich?" he said to Tessa.

"No, I've said so," Tessa said, carefully avoiding looking at him.

"In that case I'll have it. One of each please," he said to the stewardess.

Tessa stared at him in astonishment. Greedy piglet, she thought.

The stewardess looked startled but placed the two sandwiches and a coffee on a small tray, passing it over Tessa to the man and then moved on to the next seat.

He turned to Tessa, and she caught his admiring glance as he looked her up and down.

"Sorry about that," he said. "I caught the Zürich plane in a bit of a hurry and didn't get any breakfast."

Tessa shrugged, tensing up, not wishing to get into conversation. She turned again to the brochure she was reading as though this would act as a barrier between them.

He continued looking at her as he picked up his sandwich. "That's a coincidence," he said, looking down at the brochure on her lap. "Are you going to the plastics conference tomorrow? I think most people on this plane are."

Happily munching his sandwich he waved his free hand about to indicate the other passengers, while the sandwich she thought of as hers sat on his tray.

She gave a sigh and closed the brochure. "Yes, I am. What's your interest?"

"First, let me introduce myself." He looked directly at her, his grey eyes opening wide. She found his low, hypnotic voice attractive. "I'm Alex Baxter. I'm in the plastics business. I thought this conference on the future of plastics would prove interesting. How about you?"

"Tessa Corston, I'm a research lecturer. I'm involved in a five-nation project to clean up plastics in our rivers and oceans, so the future of plastics is something I really care about."

Putting his sandwich down, he wiped his fingers carefully on his napkin and offered his hand. "Hello, Tess. It's good to meet you."

As she shook his hand she felt a tingle run up and down her spine.

She let go of his hand quickly. Because calling her Tess brought back memories of Rob, who always called her that, she said angrily, "Don't call me Tess, my name is Tessa."

He recoiled as though struck with a physical blow. "Sorry,

I was just trying to be friendly."

"Well, don't," she snapped, bringing the conversation to an abrupt halt. She looked cautiously at him.

His head drooped as he pretended to study the papers on his knee. The atmosphere felt glacial.

Reaction set in as Tessa leant back in her seat, starting to feel that perhaps she had gone too far.

I'm some sort of fool to treat him like that. He hasn't done any-thing wrong. It was a gesture of friendship. Just because Rob called me Tess doesn't mean no-one else can. How can I make amends without appearing to apologise?

Taking a deep breath she leant forwards and asked, "What sort of plastics business are you in?"

His head came up immediately and the smile came back to his face. "Here take my card, this will tell you," he said. and Taking out his wallet, he handed her a gold-edged visiting card.

She glanced at the heading, *Roboplastix Inc.*

"We make plastic robots that can do all sorts of jobs around the home and also ones that can care for people."

Tessa could hear the enthusiasm in his voice. "Plastic robots? That sounds weird. How can you have a plastic robot?" Tessa was genuinely interested, her earlier anger forgotten.

"We make them from a special plastic that's as strong as steel. The robots can sweep, clean and do dozens of domestic jobs, but the caring ones are made of cuddly imitation fur."

Tessa looked quizzically at him. "Sounds interesting, but you manufacturers of plastic goods don't seem to realise what you're doing to this planet. Our project is trying to find ways of cleaning up your mess," she said, her breath quickening.

"Wow, that sounds like one heck of a project," he said with a smile.

That annoyed Tessa. She felt herself getting passionate. "It's people like you that cause the problem," she said. "So much plastic waste is being dumped in our oceans."

He looked surprised. "I doubt if our robots get dumped in the ocean—they can't swim, not yet anyway." He smiled at her. "In any case, we don't cause the problem." He took a bite of his sandwich. "It's the people who dump the plastic in the water who do the polluting."

"That may be so," Tessa said, her anger rising. She felt her cheeks flushing. She stiffened in her seat as he leant forward.

"Have you analysed how the plastics get into the rivers and oceans?" he asked.

"Yes, we have," Tessa snapped. "And in a way you're right, it's the ignorance of people throwing away unwanted plastic bottles, cling film and plastic sheets. They're the things that cause the most damage, especially when they degrade into small particles of plastic which get into our food chain from fish and other waterborne creatures."

"Stop, stop," he said, throwing up his hands. "You're giving me a lecture. Can you imagine a world without plastics?"

"Of course not." She tossed her golden hair back over her shoulders and folded her arms. "But somehow we have to stop polluting our rivers and oceans."

"It's not really my problem," he said. "But unfortunately you can't stop people doing bad things."

"You could help educate them." Tessa pounded her fist on the table making the coffee cups jump. She felt his glance again and looked away. *Huh, like all men he's so insensitive.*

As though he could read her thoughts he took another bite from his sandwich and turned back to what he was reading.

Tessa sat back. *I'm being too jumpy. I really need a break.* She thought of the conversation she'd had with her flatmate, Sandy, just before leaving. *She told me I was running away, and she was right. This conference is just an excuse. How could someone I trusted go off and have an affair with another woman? Wasn't our love enough for him? I had to get away. I'll never trust a man again, ever.*

Her thoughts were interrupted by her companion.

"Sorry, can I get by? I need to get my briefcase out of the locker. Could you hold on to this for me?" He offered his tray and half empty coffee cup.

Tessa was going to refuse, but good manners took over, and she got up, clutching both his tray and her own, coffee cups balanced precariously as she stood in the aisle letting him slide across and stand by her as he opened the overhead locker. He was tall and well built, and she was conscious of his nearness, their bodies almost touching as he stepped back and turned towards her.

He was so close that for a moment Tessa felt a crazy desire to lean forwards and put her arms round his waist. She might have done so but for the fact that she was still balancing trays with coffee cups sliding across them. He took the briefcase down, closed the locker and slid back into his seat. Feeling strange, she shook herself mentally and sat down again next to him. She leant slightly towards him, holding out his coffee. "Can you take your tray?"

Silly question. Why did I say that? He's huddled up trying to open his briefcase, there's no way he can take it.

"Could you hang on to it for just a while longer?" he asked, trying frantically to open his case.

Tessa sighed, putting both trays and coffee down on her seat table.

Successfully extracting more papers from his case he snapped it shut. "Can we repeat the process?" he asked, "I need to put it back."

Once more she juggled the trays and coffee while he slid out and placed his case in the locker.

This time, standing in the aisle, Tessa looked carefully at him. His suit was immaculate, fitting him perfectly. As he turned, his thick brown hair tumbled across his face. Tessa felt the urge to smooth it back for him. She looked at his kissable lips, his high cheekbones, then quickly looked away as he gave her a strange look, sliding back into his seat.

For the rest of the flight Tessa's thoughts were in a whirl. She was running away from a disastrous relationship, but why was she so powerfully affected by the man sitting next to her?

Gradually she relaxed. The sound of the engines, like surf rising and falling on a distant shore, lulled her to sleep. She woke with a start to find that she had fallen sideways in her seat and her head was resting comfortably on his shoulder.

"I'm so sorry," she said, straightening up as the announcement *fasten safety belts, seats in upright position* was made.

He smiled, "Don't mention it, it was rather comforting really. We are about to land. Would you like me to hold your hand?" He reached over and put her small hand in his.

Tessa was surprised but made no attempt to withdraw it as the plane lost altitude going lower and lower. Her ears popped, and finally the plane was on the ground. Rumbling and bumping along the runway, the plane taxied for what seemed ages until it came to an abrupt stop and the engines were switched off. She gently withdrew her hand, turning to him with a smile. "Thank you, that was kind of you."

Knowing how people rushed once the seat belt signs had been switched off, Tessa got up quickly to get her small case from the locker. She saw Alex trying to follow her, but a large man stood up between them and was opening the locker holding Tessa's case. When the man saw that she was pulling frantically at her case which was trapped between two others he held up his hand to stop her and lifted it down.

"There you are, my love," he said.

"Thank you." Tessa took the case, holding it in one hand, the other supporting herself on the seat behind her. She stood trapped between the mass of people all waiting for the plane door to open.

The scramble to retrieve hand luggage from the lockers continued and she became separated from Alex by a couple scrabbling to reach their suitcase and backpack crammed into one of the other lockers.

The plane door opened, and as she was pushed forwards with the flow, she turned to see Alex holding the crowd of pushing passengers back for an older lady who got stiffly out of her seat and stepped into the aisle.

He's thoughtful and kind, the absolute opposite of the one I'm running away from.

He saw her and waved, mouthing, "See you at the conference."

She nodded, tightening her coat around her as she walked past the smiling stewardesses in the doorway and out into the bright, sharp, autumn air.

The cold air caught her throat as she walked down the steps of the aircraft.

She could see Alex trying to follow her, but the crush of passengers was too great, and she lost sight of him.

Standing in the long line of passengers waiting to have their passports checked, winding like a tired snake through the long line of barriers, she looked back, but there was no sign of him. A small child pushed against her as she was slow to move forward. Eventually she reached the front of the queue waiting to put passports on the automatic system. The small child had moved away, holding its mother's hand.

She put her passport on the automatic system, but it refused to accept it. She fumbled with it as a uniformed official quickly came to her aid, putting the passport on the screen the other way round. She passed through and made her way to the baggage carousel.

People were crowding round the carousel as Tessa tried to get to the front near the moving belt. Jammed in between two large men, she suddenly became conscious of a prickly feeling in her back. She turned with difficulty and found Alex standing right behind her. As she started to speak, her suitcase came down the moving belt. She leant forwards past the largest of the men, and tried to grab it before it went past.

Alex gently moved the man out of the way.

"Here, let me," he said, as he reached for her case, swinging it easily off the moving belt. He stepped back, her suitcase in one hand and his briefcase in the other, steering himself and Tessa out of the scrum. He glanced down at her luggage label as he did so.

Handing the suitcase to her, he paused in thought for a moment, then, looked directly at her with piercing grey eyes which held her gaze in his. "If you don't mind waiting while my case comes down we could share a taxi."

Tessa shook her head regretfully. "Sorry, I wish I could, but a friend is meeting me. I'm sure we'll meet at the conference." She could see the disappointment in his eyes. *He thinks I'm meeting a man friend. I almost wish I was.*

She turned and walked away through the crowds pushing into the baggage hall.

Tessa was actually meeting Ana, a girlfriend from her schooldays. She made for the *nothing to declare* exit along with holiday makers pulling their wheeled suitcases and ushering their children in front of them.

I'm always nervous when I go through this customs area. I wonder how or when they decide to pounce on someone.

She joined the flow of people. It was obvious from the sideways glances of some of the people that they were as nervous as she was, and although she could see the two customs officials looking keenly at everyone who passed, no-one was stopped.

She walked out through the confining customs area into what she thought of as the safety of the main terminal. Standing for a moment, letting the crowd of escaping passengers flow past her, she surveyed the row of people waiting patiently behind the barrier, some looking for their loved ones, others holding boards with a person's name on, some obvious holiday couriers waiting for their flock. Then out of the mass of people, she saw Ana, looking much the same as she remembered her, her petite figure bobbing up and down to make herself visible amongst the people standing there. With her elfin-like face, she looked like one of the dolls she used to collect at school. It was Ana who had instilled a love of dolls in Tessa. She thought of the raggedy doll that she had brought with her in her suitcase, not as elegant as Ana's dolls, but still much loved.

They had kept contact for years since sharing a room at boarding school in England. When schooling had come to an end, Ana had gone back to her native Switzerland and had become an estate agent, while Tessa, after getting a degree, had stayed to get a job as a research lecturer at the University of Brookshire.

They had been so close at school that when they'd had to part there was a tremendous sense of loss. However, they kept in touch with weekly letters, then holiday visits — Tessa to Switzerland, where they went skiing in the mountains, Ana to England, where they explored the Lake District, often going farther north to the mountains and lochs of Scotland. Recently however, it had changed to emails, simply remembering birthdays and sending Christmas cards. It wasn't until Tessa decided to come to Zurich that she had emailed Ana and told her of her intention to come.

Ana's response had been immediate. "Come at once, I'm longing to see you again. It will be good to catch up on all your news."

So there she was, a little older but still the same, her face wreathed in smiles as she waved.

Tessa pushed her way through the crowd. Holding on to her small case but putting her suitcase down, she embraced Ana, kissing her on the lips.

Ana hugged her. "Come, my car is waiting." She grasped

Tessa's hand firmly. " I know you're staying at a hotel, but first we go to my apartment. I have made lunch for us."

They made their way out of the terminal to where Ana had parked her car, a little grey Citroen. As they drove off, Tessa's heart was singing at being with her friend again, her woes temporarily forgotten. She could see that Ana was also bubbling over with joy. Ana hardly stopped talking as she drove back into Zurich and then on through the crowded streets towards her apartment block, pointing out landmarks on the way.

"The Fraumunster Church, I must take you there to see the stained-glass windows, you will be also interested in the Clock and Watch museum, so much to show you." Ana drove on through the streets of Zurich.

Tessa could feel the excitement, the hustle and bustle of a live and vibrant city, people strolling, people hurrying, some just window shopping. Escaping from a bad relationship, she realised that she was looking forward to a few days with Ana and, of course, the conference.

Then, her thoughts turned to the man she had met on the plane. Now that she was free, a whole world of possibilities opened up before her. She realised that she was looking forward to meeting Alex again. Was this just fancy, or would it lead to something more?

They arrived at a newish looking apartment block.

Ana turned to her. "This is where I live. If you'll go into the lobby, I'll park the car. Take your cases, there are seats inside. Wait for me, I won't be long." She waved and drove off.

Tessa went into the entrance hall. Inside it was brightly lit and immaculately clean. The walls were painted white, and the floors were tiled in glossy black. There were plush chairs dotting the lobby and a desk in the corner where someone was working. A row of four seats faced the lift entrances. An older lady was sitting at one end hugging a shopping bag. She nodded as Tessa came in but didn't speak. Tessa sat on the seat farthest away from her, waiting.

Eventually Ana came back and took her up to the second floor, opening the door of her apartment.

Tessa paused on the threshold, looking at the neat, tidy room as Ana dragged her in.

"It is small, but I have a kitchen, a bathroom and one bedroom. Sit down, sit down, I'll get lunch then we can talk."

Tessa smiled as Ana headed for the kitchen. Ana had done nothing but talk since they'd met. She sat in one of the two easy chairs, the smell of freshly brewed coffee wafting from the kitchen. Ana emerged bearing a tray and set it down on the table under the window.

"Come," she said, pulling out a chair for Tessa to sit on.

Seated at the table, Tessa looked at the delicious plate of assorted meats, sausage, ham, cheese and fresh bread.

Ana set plates in front of them and took a bottle of red wine and two glasses from the sideboard.

"You will drink? Yes?" Before Tessa could reply, Ana had poured two glasses, handing one to Tessa.

Tessa raised her glass. "To our continued friendship."

"Santé, health and prosperity," Ana replied, clinking glasses. "Tell me your news, how is Rob?"

Tessa put down her glass. "Don't talk to me about Rob. I thought that we had an arrangement, but he cheated on me, so I left him."

Ana frowned. "Oh, Tess, that's terrible. I thought he was so good for you."

"I thought so too until I found out he was seeing another woman while I was at my evening judo class, that's when I fled. I told my flatmate if Rob came around looking for me she wasn't to tell him where I had gone."

"So you came to see me?" Ana said.

"Yes." Tessa took up her glass again. "There's also a conference on the future of plastics, but it was a wonderful opportunity to see you again."

"Are you staying for a few days?"

"Yes, I'm at the Hotel Splendide. I knew you wouldn't have room to put me up, so I decided to stay there."

"It's a very upmarket hotel. Will you have any time off from the conference?" Ana looked impressed.

"Of course, I hope we can take some trips together while I'm here. Are you still working as an estate agent?"

"Yes, four days a week. I get Friday off, so we can have a long weekend together."

"And how are your dolls? Do you still collect them?"

"Yes I do, they're in my bedroom, but I have some new ones."

Tessa detected a sadness in her tone as though something was wrong. "You sound sad. What's the matter?" she asked.

Ana looked down at her plate. "It is nothing."

They lunched in silence for a while, Ana still looking down without speaking.

Tessa stood up, went round the table and put her hand on Ana's shoulder. She bent over. "Come on Ana, you're going to have to tell me about it sooner or later. What's wrong?"

Ana looked up with tears in her eyes and clasped Tessa's hand. She took a sip of her wine and said, "It's my sweetheart, Hans." She turned and looked at Tessa as if to say *can you help?* She looked down again at her plate.

Tessa felt compassion for her friend, having just escaped from a bad situation herself. Immediately jumping to the conclusion that the same thing had happened to Ana, she said, "What happened, have you broken up with him?"

Ana looked up. "No, no, we love each other very much, it's nothing like that, it's worse."

"Worse, what could be worse?" Tessa could see Ana

getting agitated and thought perhaps that he had been involved in an accident.

Ana rose from her seat, taking her glass of wine to the window, looking out into the crowded street below.

She turned back, put her glass on the table and covered her face with her hands. "Hans has disappeared, and I don't know what to do."

Tessa put an arm round her friend's shoulders. "When did this happen?"

Ana sat down wiping tears from her eyes. "He has been gone for over a week now, and I don't know what has happened to him."

"A week isn't long. Why are you so worried?"

Ana's whole body sagged. "We have been seeing each other every day or, when he is out on a commission, as he is at the moment, he phones me twice a day, but I have heard nothing."

"Have you been to the police?" Tessa asked.

"Yes, but they didn't take it seriously. They told me that men often leave their wives and sweethearts to get a break from the stresses that can build up. They told me to come back if he hadn't turned up in a month. To them a week is nothing, but to me it is everything. I am so worried. Why has he not contacted me?" She sobbed into her handkerchief.

"Do you know where he might have gone?" Tessa leant towards her.

Ana looked up tearfully. "The last time we spoke, he said he was making dolls for a firm, something to do with plastics, I think."

Tessa sat down, surprised. "He makes dolls? "

"Yes, he is a toymaker. He made two dolls for me. Look, I will show you."

She led Tessa into her bedroom. There on the side were Ana's old dolls. Tessa went over and patted them.

"Hello old friends," she said. "They bring back some memories."

"Yes, they do, but these are the new ones." Ana pointed to two other dolls sitting on the bed. "Hans made these specially for me. They're very lifelike."

She took one carefully from the bed and handed it to Tessa. The doll was dressed in a fine brocade dress.

Tessa looked in surprise at Ana. "This doll looks just like you. He must love you very much to make it so lifelike," she said, marvelling at the detail. "And what's this?" She looked carefully at the arm of the doll, bending it and straightening it. "This is plastic, isn't it? But it looks like real skin, it's so flexible."

She looked closer, It was a type of plastic she had never seen before. Hugging the doll, she straightened its arm and handed it back to Ana, who set it back on the bed with its twin.

"That's incredible," she said. "I've never seen anything like the plastic he's used. I know we loved these other ones to bits," she waved at the collection of dolls, "but they were nothing like this. Your Hans is a very clever person."

"Yes, he is, but he is even more special to me than these dolls. What should I do?" Ana looked hopefully at her friend.

Tessa looked again from the dolls to Ana, standing there so small, so vulnerable, so tense, her brow creased with worry. She hugged her friend and Ana nestled up against her.

Then as a wave of emotion hit Tessa, they kissed. Ana was kissing her with a sort of desperation. She dragged Tessa onto the bed. "Comfort me," she said.

"Like we used to do?" Tessa asked.

"Yes, yes, I need your love." Ana slid the dress over her head and lay semi-naked reaching for Tessa, who leant forwards and kissed her, thrusting her tongue deeply into Ana's mouth. Ana pulled at Tessa's blouse undoing the buttons.

Tessa surged on to the bed while stripping off her clothes. Her hands played lightly over Ana's body, removing the rest of her clothing, caressing the small, pointed breasts. Ana closed her eyes and her body spasmed. "Is it wrong to do this?" she breathed as Tessa put her hand on Ana's stomach and felt beneath the dainty fabric.

Tessa held her tightly. "Of course not. We used to do this at school, and it shows our love for each other."

Tessa's hand moved lower, feeling the moist warmth between Ana's legs. Her hand moved rhythmically. Ana clutched at her, suddenly tensing up and then relaxing.

They lay together locked in a tender embrace as Ana's eyes closed and she slept.

Tessa lay quietly letting her friend rest, conscious that although she had given Ana an orgasm, she herself was still roused and unfulfilled. She looked down at the sleeping woman, sighed, and began to pleasure herself.

Later, Ana opened her eyes gazing lovingly at Tessa. "Thank you," she said, leaning forwards and kissing Tessa softly on the lips.

After what seemed a long time Ana urged Tessa to the bathroom. "We can shower together like we used to."

They stood together naked under the shower soaping each other's body with loving caresses, then letting the water cascade over themselves and drying each other on large fluffy towels.

After a last kiss, they dressed.

They sat for a while talking about all the trips they had taken together.

"I particularly remember our visit to Berne," Tessa said. "Wasn't that where you fell in love with that waiter?"

Ana blushed. "I don't want to remember that."

"Sorry. I forgot you are worried about Hans. I'm sure

everything is going to be all right."

"I hope so, but now I must take you to your hotel," Ana said, giving Tessa a hug. "I feel so much better now that you are here, but how can I find my sweetheart?"

Tessa thought for a moment. "Does he have a workshop and have you been there?"

Ana nodded. "He has a workshop of course. His brother Serge works with him. I have telephoned, but Serge says he does not know where Hans is."

"I'm sure there's a perfectly logical explanation." Tessa tried to reassure her. "Can you give me Hans's home address? Perhaps I could see if the people there know anything."

"That's kind of you, but it is no good, he is not there."

"Give it to me anyway, you never know, someone may know something."

"Yes, I will." Ana drew a writing pad towards her and produced a small, jewelled pen. She wrote on the pad, tearing off the sheet and handing it to Tessa.

Tessa gave her a hug. "We'll see. Tomorrow's Thursday, so after the conference I'll come and try to help you if he hasn't turned up by then."

Ana smiled. "Thank you, it is so good to have you here."

Tessa hugged her again. "It's good to be with you. Don't worry about Hans, I'm sure between us we can find him."

Ana got up. "And now I must drive you to your hotel."

"Are you sure?" Tessa asked. "I could easily get a taxi."

"No, I must take you, come."

Tessa noticed that Ana was quieter on the ride to the hotel, as though their lovemaking had reassured and calmed her.

As Ana drew up to the hotel entrance, a uniformed concierge stepped forwards and opened the car door for Tessa, who stepped out, admiring the pillared entrance. The concierge took her larger suitcase and waited while she said goodbye to Ana.

"I'll keep in touch," she said, kissing her lightly on the lips. "You mustn't worry. It will be all right."

Ana, obviously putting on a brave face, assured her that she would be fine. "I have waited a week, one more day will not make any difference, but having you here helps me a lot. See you tomorrow."

Tessa waved and Ana drove off.

As she stepped into the hotel Tessa remembered the description of the hotel which had led her to book it.

The Hotel Splendide in Zurich features classic European architecture, with its sharp angles and white stucco facade. Inside, the decor is modern, yet inviting, with marble floors, crystal chandeliers and plush velvet sofas. There is an open-air courtyard with lush gardens and a large pool surrounded by a terrace. The restaurant offers sophisticated Euro-cuisine, while the spa offers relaxing treatments like hot stone massages and manicures. It's a perfect place to escape from the hustle and bustle of city life.

She mused over this description. *The perfect place to escape from the hustle and bustle of city life and my troubles? We shall see.*

The concierge took her suitcase to the reception desk.

Looking around, Tessa was impressed by the palatial entrance hall, its pillars stretching up into the ceiling. People were milling about, some sitting, some just standing waiting. Tessa felt the throb of the hotel working like a well-oiled machine.

There was a small queue at reception and so, after waiting for her turn, she signed in with the golden pen that lay on the counter. The desk clerk smiled a false, ingratiating smile, "Welcome to the Splendide, Miss Corston. I hope you have a pleasant stay. You are in room two five seven, one of our best rooms."

He summoned a bellboy who took her up in the lift to the second floor. Opening the door of room 257, the boy put her case down and asked if there was anything more he could do for her. She tipped him, and after he had left, Tessa went over to the window, gazing out over the busy street below to the snow-capped mountains beyond.

Her old relationship left behind, a new beginning. What would the future hold?

CHAPTER TWO

As she stepped back from the window, she shivered slightly with anticipation, although the room was pleasantly warm.

She explored the spacious room with its double bed, a small sitting room leading from the main room. In the tiled bathroom the basin and bath were fitted with gleaming silver and gold taps, a walk-in shower completing the picture.

Tessa turned to the towels, large and fluffy. She felt them with approval.

Going back to the main room, she bounced up and down on the bed. She felt the pillows and was surprised at their softness. In her experience hotel pillows were usually hard and lumpy but these were so soft she looked forward to resting her head on them.

She lifted her suitcase onto the bed and began to unpack. Her first task was to set her own doll, Bella, propped against the pillows and then to put her clothes away in the wardrobe and drawers. Then, glancing in the full-length mirror, she brushed her golden hair back over her shoulders and applied simple makeup.

She had brought a limited wardrobe with her as she had worried about the weight of her case. Should she choose her silk blouse and trousers for tonight, or the elegant blue dress that brought out the sparkle in her eyes? She decided on a blouse and trousers with a simple pendant of green jade.

When it was time to go to the dining room, rather than take the lift, she walked down the grand staircase with its carved balustrade, paintings of gallant gentlemen from the past looking down on her from the walls as she passed. She made her way across the entrance hall to the dining room, where the Maître d' was standing by the reception desk.

"Ah, mademoiselle," he said, "your friend is waiting for you. I will show you to your table."

Taking a menu, he led her into the elegant room through the maze of tables, guests chattering, plates clattering, waiters in attendance.

As she followed him, her thoughts were chaotic, who could be waiting for her?

Ana was the only one she knew in Zurich.

Why is she here? she thought, then, as she was led to the table, she stopped and stepped back in surprise. It was Alex, the man from the plane.

He stood up as she approached.

The Maître d' held the chair for her and passed the menu as she sat down.

"What are you doing here?" she asked, waving the menu at him as he sat opposite her.

"I thought we might have a quiet meal together," he said with an innocent boyish look. "Get to know each other a little better before the conference."

She smiled. "All right, but our views on the future of plastics don't seem to coincide."

"That doesn't matter, I promise to be good," he said, taking the menu from her and placing it on the table. "Before you choose, I suggest a glass of champagne?"

Feeling slightly overwhelmed Tessa nodded.

A waiter hovered behind them.

"Alphonse, two glasses of Louis Roederer Cristal Brut," he said.

"I would recommend the two thousand and eight vintage," the waiter suggested.

"Excellent, thank you, Alphonse."

"You see I am well looked after here," he said as the champagne was brought.

He raised his glass. "To us." They clinked glasses.

"I'm not sure about that," Tessa said, gazing attentively at the bubbles in her glass.

Then she looked up, fixing him with her gaze. "I don't generally drink champagne with someone I don't know." She smiled. "Who are you? Could you tell me something about yourself?"

He toyed with his napkin, "I've told you. I'm in the plastics business. We are both going to the conference, so I thought we should get to know each other a little better, that's all."

Is it? I wonder. She looked carefully at him. *He is rather dishy in a reckless, devil may care sort of way. His brown hair is showing a little white at the temples, his suit immaculate.*

She took a large drink from her glass to cover her confusion.

"No, no," he said, putting out his hand to steady her. "Champagne of this vintage is made to be sipped, not drunk like water."

Tessa laughed, putting her glass down as he withdrew his hand. "Sorry, I was miles away."

"Well then, you must come back to the present and choose what you would like to eat."

He passed her the menu. "I come here fairly often, so I can say that everything is good."

Tessa looked down the menu, then putting it aside, said, "So you're not staying at the hotel?"

"No, I have a place of my own, but I like to come here, the food is excellent. What will you have?"

She picked up the menu again, glancing through it. "It's difficult to choose. Since you're a regular here, what do you suggest?"

"We'll let our waiter order for us, he knows my tastes and

I'm sure it will suit you, unless there is anything special you want?"

"No, I rely on you."

Alex turned to the waiter who was standing behind his chair. "Well, Alphonse, what should it be tonight?"

Alphonse took the menu from him with a smile. "Tonight I would recommend the turbot, chef had it fresh today. Perhaps you would like to start with the soup, a bouillabaisse?"

"Sounds excellent." Alex looked at Tessa. "Would that be all right?"

Tessa was relieved at not having to make a choice. "That's fine." She sat back in her chair looking again at this handsome man, trying to analyse her feelings.

"And the wine, Alphonse?" Alex turned to Tessa. "They have an excellent Chablis."

"Yes, monsieur, I would have suggested it myself." He bowed, taking the menus.

Tessa looked around. The dining room was full, mainly couples, but nearby sat a party of four, and over in the corner a party of six, obviously a birthday celebration. The noise level began to mount, but there seemed no need for conversation as Tessa relaxed and began to enjoy herself.

The meal was excellent. The bouillabaisse, the turbot were delicious, and Tessa felt a glow spreading through her body.

The waiter handed them the dessert menu. "I would recommend strawberries and cream," he said.

"Excellent. All right for you?" Alex looked at Tessa who nodded.

The dessert arrived, the waiter asking if they would like coffee afterwards.

"Black for me," Tessa said.

"For me also. Perhaps you would like to take it in the lounge?" Alex asked.

"That will be fine." Then, she glanced at the delicious bowl of strawberries. "These look absolutely gorgeous."

Savouring the last mouthful, Tessa sat back. "A wonderful meal Alex, thank you." She had to almost shout as the noise level had risen even more now that the evening had got into full swing.

Alex leant across and took her hand. "Come, let's go to the lounge, it is quieter there and more comfortable."

Tessa let him lead her into the lounge, which was quiet and spacious, with settees and easy chairs spaced far enough apart so that people could conduct a private conversation without being overheard, although there would be no fear of that as it was half empty.

When they were seated side by side in the dimly lit atmosphere, he asked, "Would you like a brandy with your coffee?"

Tessa held up her hand. "No thank you. The wine was superb, but I think that's enough alcohol for tonight."

Alex smiled. "You don't mind if I have one? I find it finishes off the meal."

"Of course not." Tessa felt strangely content.

I haven't felt so companionable with a man for such a long time. I wonder how he feels about me.

Alex began to talk about his background, how his favourite toy had been a plastic bunny that waggled it's ears and walked along the tabletop.

"That's probably what sparked my interest in plastics," he said, laughing. "It might even explain my interest in robots. But that's enough about me. How about you?"

Tessa felt his gaze taking in every aspect of her, her golden hair, her slim body. She suddenly felt exposed.

To cover her confusion she said, "There's not much to tell, really. My father is the vicar in a small parish near Tunbridge Wells. My mother supports him and is a staunch member of the local Women's Institute. I went to a fairly conventional boarding school in the area. That was where I met my best friend, Ana. She now lives and works in Zurich. I ought to have explained properly when we met getting our cases. That was why I couldn't share a taxi with you. She was meeting me to go for lunch in her flat."

She could see a sudden surge of relief in his face.

Now he knows it wasn't a man I was meeting,

Tessa tried to think of what else she could tell him, then she remembered Ana's dolls.

"We both have a love of dolls going back to school days. Ana used to collect them. I thought she had grown out of it, although she still has her collection, but while I was there to-day she showed me two dolls that her sweetheart Hans had made for her. He's a toymaker, and the dolls she showed me were exquisite. There's something there that might interest you. They were made of a plastic I've never seen before. You probably know about this type of plastic already, it was so real, like human skin, flexible and lifelike."

Alex put his coffee down and looked at her with immediate interest.

"Lifelike plastic skin," he said. "Now that is interesting, I wonder who makes it? I've never heard of such a thing, but it could have many important applications, especially for our robots. Perhaps we shall find out tomorrow at the conference."

Sipping her coffee, Tessa looked again at Alex. In the dim light, his high cheekbones were accentuated, and his eyes seemed to gleam with enthusiasm.

She sensed a change in him. Was he interested in the new plastic, or was he interested in her?

A waiter came up to them. "Excuse me, are you Miss Corston?" Tessa nodded. "There is a telephone call for you. You can take it over there if you wish." He indicated a small alcove on the left of where they were sitting.

Alex leant back in his seat. The gleam died out of his eyes.

The moment was over.

Tessa wriggled in her chair. "Who on earth can it be? No one knows I'm here except Ana."

"No boyfriends chasing you?" Alex looked thoughtfully at her.

Tessa laughed. "No boyfriends. Not now, anyway."

Alex got up politely as she left to go to the phone and then settled back with his brandy and coffee.

Tessa picked up the phone. It was Ana. An Ana who was almost incoherent. "One of my dolls has gone," she said, her voice choking as she spoke.

Tessa realised that Ana was trying to get a grip on herself.

"Calm down," she said. "Tell me exactly what happened. Are you all right?"

"I'm all right but a bit scared. I was just settling down to watch television when there was a ring at the doorbell, I answered it to a man I've never seen before. He pushed his way into my apartment, nearly knocking me over, grabbed my arm, and asked *Where are they?* I said *What are you talking about?* I felt dreadful and shaky. He said *The dolls, of course. Never mind, I'll find them.* He pushed me away and tramped through the room, first opening the bathroom door, then the kitchen, and finally my bedroom door. He looked round, saw the dolls on the side, and picked one up, examining it carefully. Then, while I looked through the bedroom door to see what he was doing, he knocked them all on the floor and turned to the bed where Hans's dolls were sitting. He took one look, grabbed them both and pushed me out of the way. I tried to stop him, but he was too strong. I beat my fists against him with all my might, and he dropped one of the dolls as he ran out of the apartment. It seems crazy, but all he seemed to want were the dolls Hans had made. Why would he want to steal them? It doesn't make sense."

Tessa thought for a moment. "Do you think it has anything

to do with Hans's disappearance? The dolls you showed me were pretty special, at least their plastic skin was."

"Oh, I don't know." Ana sounded desperate. "Do you think you could come over to be with me for a while? I don't want to be alone. I'm scared he may come back."

"Of course I'll come," Tessa said without hesitation. "I'll get a taxi and be there as soon as I can."

Going back to Alex, she apologised. "I'm sorry but I have to leave."

Disappointment showed on his face. Rising from his chair he asked, "What's wrong? I was so enjoying our evening together."

"It's my friend Ana. She's had something stolen. I must go to her."

Alex looked as though he was going to suggest that he go along, but instead he bent forwards and held her hand. "Can I see you tomorrow at the conference?"

The warmth of his hand felt good and natural. Reluctantly, she drew away. "I would like that. Until tomorrow then, but now I must go."

Inside she was full of conflicting feelings. This man was affecting her in some way that she didn't understand. She felt the tug of friendship for Ana, but with Alex it was something more. She hurried away, Alex standing looking after her as she hurried into the reception area.

She asked the concierge to call her a taxi, and it was only when she got into the taxi that she realised that she hadn't arranged when and where to meet with Alex. She felt she couldn't go back and ask him.

She arrived at Ana's apartment, rang the bell, and called through the door, "Ana, it's me," realising that she might be frightened unless she knew who the caller was.

When Ana opened the door, Tessa could tell that she was

very upset. She let Tessa in, closing the door rapidly and bolting it.

Her face was pale and her hair dishevelled. She was hugging the one remaining doll. She threw herself into Tessa's arms, holding her tight. "Thank you for coming. I was so frightened. Why would anyone want to steal my dolls?"

"I don't know," Tessa said, stroking Ana's hair, "but it's all right now."

"I was really afraid he might come back for the other doll."

"You must tell the police. Have you phoned them?"

"No, they were so unhelpful about Hans. What's the point?"

"Well, I'm sure nothing else will happen," Tessa reassured her. "What was he like, this man?"

"It all happened so quickly. He was big and rough. Certainly very strong. I don't really know," Ana, still clutching her doll, was shaking terribly.

Tessa sat her down. "Look, I'm going to make some tea." She held up her hand as Ana made to rise. "No, don't worry. I'm sure I can find my way around your kitchen."

The tea seemed to calm Ana, and after some time she said, "I'm all right now, Tess. You must get back to your hotel."

"I think I ought to stay for a while," Tessa said, looking at her friend's worried face.

Gradually Ana began to relax as they talked about past holidays and things they had done together.

Suddenly there was a knock on the door.

Ana raised her hands to her face. "It's him. What shall we do?"

"I'll answer the door, don't worry it may not be him." Tessa went to the door and opened it.

A large man stood there holding a package.

"What's this?" Tessa asked. "Special delivery," he said.

"Thank you." Tessa held out her hand.

The man grabbed it and twisted her arm behind her back. "I don't know who you are," he said, "but I've come for the doll I dropped."

As he went forwards with her into the room, Ana cried out, "It's him! That's the man that stole my doll."

"And I'm going to take the other one," he said, releasing Tessa's arm and pushing her down onto a chair.

"You stay there. I don't want any trouble, but I do need the other doll. Where is it?" He turned to Ana. "Ah, there it is." He spotted it on the table where Ana had laid it down. As he grabbed it, Tessa launched herself at him. He was hampered by trying to hold the package and the doll. Tessa got him in a judo hold and he crashed to the floor. Tessa tried to hold him down, but he was too powerful. He wriggled free, got to his feet and staggered out of the door, leaving the package and the doll on the floor where he had dropped them. Breathing heavily, Ana rushed over, locking and bolting the door as Tessa collapsed onto a chair.

"Are you all right?" Ana asked, going over to her. "That was very brave of you," she said, her voice quavering.

"I'll be fine in a minute," Tessa said. "Let me get my breath back. At least we saved your doll. I wonder what's in the package?" She picked it up and opened it. " It's just newspaper inside a brown paper bag. Just something to get him inside." She took it to the kitchen, and threw it in the bin.

Ana picked her doll off the floor where it had been dropped and placed it carefully on the table, smoothing its dress down and patting its hair.

They both sat for a while lost in thought, looking at the doll, until Tessa looked at her watch. "Goodness, is that the time. Would you like me to stay with you tonight?"

"No, I'll be fine," Ana said. "But I'm going to lock my door carefully after you've gone."

Tessa looked at her friend. "I don't think he'll try again.

Will you let me phone the police?"

"What's the point? He's gone and he's got one of the dolls, there's nothing they can do."

Tessa looked thoughtful. "It must be something to do with Hans and the special plastic, otherwise how would he know about your dolls?"

Ana said tearfully, "I don't know what's so special about my dolls."

"It's a mystery, but don't worry, we'll solve it together. Now, are you sure you don't want me to stay?"

"No, really, I'll be all right."

"Well, if you're sure. I'll be back tomorrow after the conference."

"Not too early, as I shall be at work until five." Ana had regained colour in her face. She hugged Tessa again.

As Tessa went out through the front door of Ana's apartment she could hear her locking the door and putting the security catch on. "See you soon," she called through the door.

Going down in the lift, she wondered if Alex would be still there when she got back.

On the street, she looked round nervously, but there was no sight of the intruder. She gave a sigh of relief as a taxi came into sight. She hailed it, directing the driver to the Hotel Splendide.

Concentrating on Ana's problem had for the moment stopped Tessa thinking about Alex, but in the taxi, it all flooded back. Daydreaming, she imagined they were walking along the bank of a stream holding hands. He turned and pulled her to him with a long lingering kiss.

"Your hotel, mademoiselle," The taxi driver opened the door, rousing her from her daydream.

She paid him and made her way into the vast reception area, pausing for a moment to look in the dining room which still contained a few guests, but Alex had gone.

The Maître d' hurried up to her. "Can I help you, mademoiselle? I regret that Monsieur Baxter has gone back to his chateau, but he left you this note." He passed her a folded piece of paper.

She turned away and opened it.

My dear Tessa, I hope your friend is all right. I realised after you left that we hadn't arranged where to meet tomorrow. There is a coffee bar just outside the lecture rooms on the first floor of the conference hall. Could we meet there at 11 o'clock after your first lecture? Alex.

She read it again. Was there just a suspicion that the *x* in his name had been turned into a kiss? No, it was stupid to imagine that. She folded the paper, thanked the Maître d', and hurried to the second floor.

Back in her room, she looked at herself in the mirror. Why was this man disturbing her feelings so much? She admitted to herself that she was looking forward to seeing him again, perhaps more than she was looking forward to the conference itself.

Tessa slept well and woke on Thursday morning with the pleasant feeling of something to look forward to.

Putting on her business suit, she went down to the dining room. There were one or two couples, but the dining room was mainly full of earnest looking men dressed in sober suits, obviously there for the conference.

Tessa sat alone and had her usual breakfast of orange juice, croissant, fruit compote, toast and cheese, followed by a cup of black coffee.

Alex kept coming back into her mind as she looked at the motley collection of males. Why should Alex affect her so much when these men didn't? That was a question she couldn't answer.

When she was back in her room she cleaned her teeth, checked her makeup, picked up her handbag, and went to the lift. As she came out on the ground floor, people were hurrying in all directions.

She asked the concierge to call a taxi, and as it came, two men hurried up to her.

"Are you going to the conference? Could we share your taxi? We're very late and we have to get there quickly to be on our stand," one asked.

Tessa turned and looked at them—obviously professionals, they didn't look threatening. She made a quick decision and waved them into the car. 'Feel free. Yes, I am going, it's no problem."

In the taxi they introduced themselves as Ted Clapton and Fred Jackson, one tall and thin, the other short and round. Fred was the jollier of the two, Ted seeming more the serious academic type. Fred explained that their company produced equipment to clean up waste from the oceans.

"That's a coincidence, it's my interest as well," Tessa said.

Fred pressed a business card into her hand. "In that case, you must come and see our stand. Later we're arranging demonstrations on the river of how the system works, if you would like a boat ride?"

"I'd like that." Tessa put the card in her handbag.

When they reached the conference hall, Fred insisted on paying the taxi.

"Don't worry, it's on expenses," he said as they hurried off through the exhibitors entrance, leaving Tessa to show her invitation card at the visitor's reception desk. She was given a copy of the programme, which contained details of the lectures and also information about the various stands in the exhibition area.

As Tessa walked into the main hall she was overwhelmed by the vastness of it. There were stands everywhere, advertising all manner of plastic wares. The colours almost blinded the eye, and the lighting was so bright it made Tessa wish she had brought dark glasses.

It was quite early, and many of the stands were still being set up. There weren't many visitors yet, so the hall wasn't very crowded, and Tessa had time to look around before her first lecture. The lecture rooms were on the first floor.

She could see from her programme that the Roboplastix Inc stand was situated in the middle of the hall. As she approached, she saw that it was large, occupying a double space measured against some of the nearby stands. To her surprise, she saw Alex talking to two people on the stand, obviously assistants.

Her heart quickened as she came up to him.

As if he sensed her presence he turned and greeted her. "Tessa, you came early?" Then to the people he was talking to, "Excuse me, this is a friend, I'll be with you again in a minute."

He put his hand on her shoulder. "And how is your friend?" he asked.

As he touched her, a thrill ran through her body. She remembered her daydream in the taxi. She couldn't bring herself to look in his eyes in case she saw something that might upset the dream.

She gently moved away from him. "I haven't spoken to Ana today. You remember I told you about the dolls made with the special plastic? She had one stolen last night, that was why she phoned me," she said, her voice unsteady. To regain her balance she turned to look at the stand and for a moment couldn't believe what she saw.

The exhibit was a mock-up of a kitchen. In it, two large

dolls were moving about. One was vacuuming the floor, the other was washing clothes. Both had beautifully sculpted faces.

"They're our domestic robots," Alex said as she stared at them. "We make them small with appealing faces so their owners will take to them. I call them our little dolls. The toymaker, Hans, modelled the faces for us."

"So this is your stand, and you knew about the toymaker, Hans?" she looked at him in surprise.

Alex looked shamefaced. "Yes, I told you on the plane, I'm part owner of Roboplastix Inc. I was going to tell you about Hans last night, but after you took your phone call, everything happened so quickly.

"You employed Hans to make these dolls and you knew about him?" Tessa repeated slowly as though she couldn't believe it.

Alex stepped back as though to defend himself, "It's not quite like that."

Tessa turned to him. "Then you must have known last night that Hans was missing, and you must also have known about the new plastic. Why didn't you tell me? Perhaps you knew the dolls were going to be stolen?" Tessa felt herself becoming angry, her face colouring up. She walked quickly away.

"Wait." Alex hurried after her. "Let me explain."

Tessa was furious. "What is there to explain?" She faced him. "And what have you done with Hans?"

"Please, let me explain," he repeated, putting his hand on her shoulder.

She shook it off angrily. "I must go to my lecture."

"At least meet me afterwards as we arranged."

She took one look at his hangdog expression. "Maybe," she said as she walked away.

33

Tessa went up and found the first-floor lecture room already filled with people. She sat at the back and to the side so she could get away quickly. The lecture was informative, but she had already heard most of the arguments before, and her mind was whirling at the turn of events.

The lecture finished with enthusiastic applause as Tessa slid out of her seat and headed for the exit. She found her feet taking herself to the coffee bar in spite of herself. She walked into the mass of people talking, eating, and gossiping. No sign of Alex, so she bought herself a coffee and a squidgy comfort cake at the counter, found a vacant table, and sat down. Her whole being felt shaken. She had begun to have so much trust in this man and now it was all shattered.

Of course he'll be late. I'll wait ten minutes, and then if he isn't here, I'll go.

It wasn't quite ten minutes. He appeared from the crowd and sat opposite her carrying his coffee.

He set the coffee down, then leaned across the table and tried to hold her hand.

She brushed it away irritably.

"Will you let me explain?"

Grudgingly, Tessa nodded.

Alex took his coffee cup in both hands twirling it round. "I know nothing about this new plastic, if it exists at all. I was as surprised as you were when you told me about it."

"Well, I can prove to you about the plastic, as Ana still has one of the dolls. If Hans made these dolls for you, where is he, and who stole one of Ana's dolls?"

Alex put his cup down and held up his hand. "Hold on a second. First, I don't know where Hans is. As far as I know, once he had done the work for us, he left. As to the theft of the doll, I had nothing to do with that, but I would be interested in seeing this new plastic, as it might be just what we need to make our robots seem more human."

Perhaps he is more interested in the plastic than me? Should I let him see Ana's doll? He may even have sent the other man to steal it and is now trying a different approach.

CHAPTER THREE

Tessa looked at him carefully. Today he was dressed in a rich brown sports jacket and slacks, with a white silk shirt open at the neck. *He looks so innocent, but men are such liars. How can I trust him and yet I still feel this attraction to him?*

As though Alex sensed her feelings, he leant across the table taking both her hands in his. "I want you to trust me, I will help you any way I can. What more can I say?"

Tessa jerked her hands away, picked up and crushed her empty paper coffee cup. "It sounds as though you don't know what's going on in your own firm," she said crossly.

Alex looked nervously at her. "As you know, I've been in England. I leave my partner to keep things running while I'm away," he began. "I'll ask him about the toymaker tomorrow, but in any case, I would like to see the doll you're telling me about. Can you arrange it?"

Tessa looked at him critically. *Is it safe to take him to Ana or is this just another way to get hold of more of the special plastic as the other attempt had failed? Am I being paranoid about this?*

She decided to trust him. "Meet me at the Splendide at six o'clock tonight. I'll try to arrange it with Ana. If I can't arrange it, I'll phone. Can I have your mobile number?"

"Good idea, let's exchange numbers so we can keep in touch."

That wasn't very clever, she thought. Now he'll have my number. But she fished in her handbag and opened her diary. "I never remember my number. Ah, here it is."

Alex wrote it down, then took his visiting card and

scribbled his own number on the back. "I hope you can ar-range it. Let me know if you can't, but now I must get back to the stand." He got up and made off through the crowded café, leaving Tessa wondering if she had done the right thing.

She rang Ana on her mobile.

"I've found out that Hans was working for a firm called Roboplastix Inc. The boss is Alex Baxter, I talked to him about the theft of your doll, and he asked if he could see the doll you still have as he's interested in the plastic."

"I'm not sure," Ana said nervously. "Is it just a trick to get the other doll?"

"I don't think so," Tessa said reassuringly. "I met him on the plane coming over, and in any case he was having dinner with me last night when you had your intruder so he couldn't have been involved."

"He's your new boyfriend?" Ana laughed.

"Not really." Tessa blushed. Thank goodness Ana couldn't see her face.

"Would it be all right to bring him over after about six o'clock? He might have some news on Hans's whereabouts."

"That's fine, I'd like to meet your new boyfriend."

"He's not . . . Thanks Ana, I'll bring him over."

Tessa felt she must go to the next lecture, which was the special one on the future of plastics, but the speaker didn't hold her attention. There were two or three hundred people present, but Tessa found her thoughts revolving round the events of the day. She came back to earth as the speaker rounded off the talk by saying, "The world will always need plastics, so the future is ours."

As Tessa left the lecture room, her thoughts were on her own future, but she thought she ought to have a look at some of the stands before she left for the day.

She walked down the stairs to the ground floor. The noise of hundreds of people talking hit her like a solid wall. As she walked around the stands she became aware of two men waving at her from a stand displaying a mess of old plastic bottles and other plastic debris. They were the men she had shared the taxi with, Ted and Fred.

She went over to their stand, which showed a sandy beach littered with plastic waste.

"You said you were interested in cleaning up plastic waste?" Fred looked at her quizzically.

"Yes, I'm involved with a five-nation project on the subject."

Fred smiled. "That's a coincidence—we're trying to interest them in our ideas. Look, why don't you come to see our demonstration on the River Limmat, Saturday?" He handed her a printed sheet with the details.

Tessa glanced at it. "Yes, I'd like to." Then she had a thought. "Is it all right if I bring a friend?"

"The more the merrier. See you on the river. We start from the pier at ten am. The boat is called *Friends of Fish*."

"That's a good name," Tessa said approvingly. "I'll certainly be there, hopefully with a friend. Before I go, can you tell me anything about a firm called Roboplastix Inc?"

"Where did you find out about them?" Ted said. "That's a pretty powerful outfit. They're big in Zurich. Main offices are in the Barnstrasser, and they have a research centre at the top of one of the mountains round here somewhere. What's your interest?"

If only you knew. Tessa smiled inwardly. "Thanks, I think I'll take a look at their stand. It's just that their name came up in conversation."

"See you on Saturday," Fred said. "Don't be late."

They waved goodbye.

As Tessa wandered off, she thought it would be good if she could persuade Alex to come to this demonstration. It might open his eyes to the problem of plastic waste.

People had now flooded into the hall, and the Roboplastix stand was surrounded by a large number of people.

Tessa pushed through the crowd to get to the front. The small doll-like robots were still performing domestic tasks. Tessa went up to one of the robots and touched its arm.

An assistant hurried up to her. "Sorry, please don't touch the exhibits."

Tessa backed away, satisfied that the material was nothing like the plastic she had seen on Ana's dolls. It was just some form of solid bluish plastic.

As she turned away, the assistant said, "Can I help you?"

"No, thank you, I was just admiring your exhibits."

"They are rather good, aren't they," the assistant said enthusiastically. "I wish I could take one home with me. Have you seen our comfort robots? You can touch them."

"No, what are they?"

The assistant took what looked like a large cuddly bear from the table on the side and thrust it into Tessa's arms. It immediately spoke, asking, "How are you today?"

Tessa almost dropped it in surprise.

"It's all right, you can talk to it. It's designed to be a companion for the elderly or people who are ill."

Tessa examined the bear carefully. It looked like a teddy bear and had soft fluffy brown fur. As she was turning it in her hands it said again, "How are you today?"

"I'm fine," Tessa said, feeling foolish talking to a bear.

"I'm glad to hear that," it said. "Have a nice day."

Tessa handed it back carefully. "Nice. Can it say other things?"

"Oh, yes, it's got quite a vocabulary. Do you want to hear some more?"

Tessa shook her head. "No thanks, but it's an interesting idea."

As she turned to look at the robot dolls again, Alex came

out from the back of the stand.

"You came back?"

"Yes, these robot dolls are really amazing, and I've just been introduced to your cuddly bear."

"We've got quite a range of cuddly animals as well as the robots, but did you manage to fix our visit to your friend?"

"Meet me at six in the hotel foyer, we can go to see her then. Do you have any news about Hans?"

"Not yet, I can't get hold of my partner. I'm going back to the office this afternoon, so I should be able to find out something then. I'll let you know when we meet."

Tessa was just about to turn away when she remembered, "Before I forget, I've got another surprise for you. How about coming with me on Saturday for a boat trip?"

"What's this?" Alex looked surprised. "Are you asking me out on a date?"

"Not exactly a date, but there's a demonstration on cleaning up plastic waste at the River Limmat at ten o'clock on Saturday. I thought it might do you good to see what's being done to clear up your waste."

"It's not my waste," he said in a carefully controlled voice. "Yes, I'll come. Where is it?"

"At the pier. It starts from there at ten o'clock. The boat's called *Friends of Fish*."

"What a funny name."

"Yes, well, we English are a funny lot."

"I'm English as well, you know." Alex looked affronted, "My mother is English. She lives in Sussex. My father is Swiss. He started this firm with a friend. When he died, I took it over jointly with the friend's son. I didn't want to, and I certainly didn't want a partner. I was a chartered accountant, but I did it for my mother, and so far it has worked out all right."

This is a good man. But she said aloud, "You must love her very much to give up your career."

Alex looked down. "It took a lot of thought but . . ." He looked up. "Now I've done it, I'm quite proud of what we've achieved."

Looking at the large stand, Tessa said, "And rightly so. You should be proud. Anyway, first meet me tonight at six. We'll go to see Ana's doll." She waved goodbye.

Leaving Alex, her thoughts turned again to Ana and her missing sweetheart. *I've got the afternoon free. Why don't I see if I can find Hans myself? Now where is that address Ana gave me?*

She scrabbled in her handbag and pulled out the crumpled piece of paper.

From the exit, she hailed one of the taxis waiting outside. The taxi driver spoke no English, so she showed him the address Ana had written, he nodded, and they were off.

They travelled to an older part of the city, where they arrived in a scruffy street with houses on either side leaning perilously towards each other. She gave the driver the money shown on the meter and was wondering if she should tip him when he took the money and drove off rapidly as though afraid of staying a moment longer.

She checked the address and walked towards the row of buttons on the wall outside an old apartment building. Half of the buttons had no name on them, and she couldn't find one labelled Hans Richter, but the bottom one said *Manager*, so she pushed it. The door catch buzzed, and she went into the smell of fried onion and sausage. On the left a door was marked *Manager*. She knocked, and to her surprise a young woman with long blonde plaits wearing a traditional costume came out and looked questioningly at her.

"Guten Morgen," she said, smiling.

"Good Morning," replied Tess.

"Oh, you are English. How can I help you?"

"I'm looking for Hans Richter. I believe he lives here?"

The woman looked worried. "Yes, he has a room on the

first floor, but we have not seen him now for over a week."

"Do you know where he might have gone?"

"I am sorry, but no. You might try his workshop. It's in the next street on the left, in a café called *The House of Dolls.* You can't miss it."

Tessa thanked her, wondering if she could find it, but she followed the directions and there was the café. A newly painted sign above the door declared that it was indeed *The House of Dolls,* and in the window were dolls dressed in traditional costumes.

This couldn't be right. What would a toymaker's workshop be doing in a café? She entered and walked up to the counter. A shelf ran round the walls, and on it were small dolls, miniatures of the ones that Hans had given to Ana.

"I see you are looking at the dolls." A jolly looking man with an apron tied round his ample middle smiled at her.

"Yes, I was, but I was told that Hans Richter had a workshop here. This is a café — it can't be a workshop?"

"Ah, but he has a shed in the back. You like his dolls?" He waved his hand round the room."

Tessa glanced round. "Yes, I recognise his work. I've seen dolls like this before. Is he in at the moment?"

The man's expression changed. "No, we haven't seen him for a week or so ,but his brother comes in regularly each day, and he's there now. Would you like to go through to the shed?" He held the counter flap open for her.

The way to the shed was through a small kitchen and out the back door to a dilapidated wooden building. Tessa stood at the open door of the shed and looked in.

A young man was bent over a lathe. He looked up and saw her standing there. Shutting off the power, he beckoned her in.

"What can I do for you?" he asked, rubbing his hands on a greasy cloth. "Old Bartoll doesn't usually let people through to see us. You must have impressed him. I'm Serge." He shook hands.

"I'm Tessa," she said. "I've come to see your brother. Is he in?"

"Haven't seen him for a while. Sometimes he goes away if he gets a commission. This time it must have been a big one, as he isn't usually away this long. Can I help? Look, it's about my break time. Come and have a coffee with me."

They went back into the café and sat at one of the tables. Herr Bartoll came over and asked them what they wanted. Serge looked at Tessa.

"Just coffee please," she said.

"Two coffees then," Serge said.

Tessa looked around the room. Apart from two couples on the other side of the room, the café was empty.

"How do you like the dolls?" Serge asked. "They were my idea. Hans had a large consignment of dolls cancelled, so I suggested we give them to Bartoll. He was delighted and put them all round the walls, as you can see."

Their coffee arrived. "I was just talking about your dolls," Serge said.

"Ja, I changed the name of the café because of them. You like?"

"I think they're great," Tessa said, sipping her coffee.

Herr Bartoll smiled happily and went away to serve another customer.

"You help your brother with his work?" she asked Serge.

"Yes, I like helping him, but my real interest is in racing cars. I can't afford to get into that yet, but I've tuned up the engine of my old car so that it behaves like one."

Tessa could feel his enthusiasm. *He looks a likeable young man. About my age.*

She took in his youthful figure, his innocent looking face flushed with enthusiasm.

"I've got my car outside. Where are you staying? I could

give you a ride back. if you like."

Tessa felt nervous after hearing about his car, but she said, "That's kind of you. I'm staying at a hotel fairly nearby. Don't worry, I can easily get a taxi back. But first, what about your brother? Do you know where he is?"

Serge looked down at his coffee. "I wish I did. I'm getting worried about him."

"Have you any idea where he might be?" she asked.

Serge thought for a moment. "His last contact was with a plastics firm, but why they were interested in dolls, I don't know."

"Do you have their address?"

"It's back in the workshop. I can get it if you like."

"Yes, please," Tessa said, leaning back.

While he was gone Herr Bartoll came over. "A fine boy that, mad about cars, but he keeps his brother's work going while he is away."

He turned and called, "Coming, coming," as one of the couples waved at him.

Serge came back with a scrap of paper. "Here it is, a firm called Roboplastix Inc. They've got a big office block in the Barnstrasser."

Tessa took the paper. "Thanks, that confirms what I thought."

Serge looked at her. "What's your interest?"

Tessa, not sure how to answer, said, "I'm a friend of Ana's. She's worried about Hans as she hasn't heard from him. I want to help her if I can."

"I understand." Serge picked up his coffee. "Ana is a good person. I spoke to her recently, and I know she is worried about Hans. Look, if he turns up, would you like me to phone you?" He then seemed to hesitate. "Um, better still, could I see you again?"

Not another one! Tessa looked critically at him. *He is quite attractive. After I've taken Alex to see Ana, he's bound to want to*

44

continue on to dinner. I'm not committed to him, so I'm free if I want to go out with someone else instead.

Without thinking it out properly, she said impulsively, "How about dinner tonight? You could tell me all about your brother."

Serge looked like the young man he was. His face flushed with pleasure. "That would be great. Do you like pasta?"

She smiled at him. "I love pasta."

"I know this place where they serve terrific pasta. Can I pick you up at eight o'clock?"

"Make it eight thirty, I've got an appointment earlier, but I should be back by then. I'm staying at the Splendide."

"Wow, that's some hotel," Serge said, visibly impressed. "Okay, let me drive you back."

They went to where Serge's car was parked. Tessa could tell as soon as Serge switched on the engine and revved up that she was right to feel nervous. Even though she had a seat belt, the way that Serge drove, speeding up on the corners, racing down the straights, made her glad when they reached the hotel.

A little shakily she got out of the car and waved as he roared away.

Tessa took the rest of the afternoon off, reading *Devil's Destiny*, the romantic book she'd brought with her. She had just got to the part where the hero snatches the heroine up on his horse and gallops off into the sunset when she realised she'd had little to eat that day, so she went down and ordered a cream tea.

Sitting quietly in the lounge, which seemed strangely cold and bleak in the afternoon light, she felt she was wrong to go out with Serge but then justified it by thinking that it would do Alex good to know that he wasn't the only man around.

At five to six, Tessa went down into the foyer of the hotel. As she walked towards the entrance Alex came in. He greeted her with a kiss on the cheek.

"I've got my car outside."

Tessa followed him out into the cold sharp air, and there was a chauffeured limousine waiting for them.

Tessa slid into the warm interior of the back seat, Alex sitting beside her as she gave Ana's address to the driver.

Ana was waiting for them. She shook hands with Alex a little nervously, hugging Tessa.

"This is my friend Ana," Tessa said. "Alex Baxter, Ana. He has a firm making plastic robots."

Ana looked surprised but didn't comment. Instead she said, "Come in, come in."

She had laid the table with a variety of cheeses, biscuits, and nibbles. She took their coats through to the bedroom, motioning them to sit down. "Will you have some wine?"

Tessa could see that Alex was dying to ask what sort, but out of politeness he just nodded and said, "Thank you."

Ana served the wine and offered biscuits and cheese.

Conversation was a little difficult at first, but then as Ana began to relax, Alex brought up the subject of the robbery.

"I was sorry to hear of the theft of your doll," he said. "I believe it was one of a pair made for you by the toymaker we employed."

"Yes," Ana looked concerned. "Hans is a great friend of mine, but he seems to have disappeared. Is he still working for you?"

Alex didn't answer at first, instead picking up his wine and taking a sip. "This is good. What is it by the way?"

"It's a Sauvignon," Ana said absently, "but do you have any news of Hans?"

"I'm sorry, no, nothing other than he was employed by my partner, Eric Weber, who will be at the exhibition tomorrow. Why don't you come and see my dolls? I can give you a pass, and you can ask him about Hans yourself."

Ana looked puzzled. "Yes, I would like that, but you have dolls also?"

Alex smiled. "Well, we call them dolls. They're really small robots that can do all sorts of domestic tasks."

"Don't forget your comfort robots," Tessa said, turning to Ana. " They've got this cuddly bear that talks."

"Yes, it's one of a range of robots specially designed to be companions for elderly people. We've got bears, cats and quite a range of animals," Alex said proudly. "But what about your doll? Tessa tells me it's very special to you."

Ana turned to Tessa, "Is it all right to show it to him?"

"Yes, I've told Alex all about it. Let him see it."

Ana went into her bedroom and brought out the doll, its blue eyes staring at Alex, its golden hair slightly dishevelled.

"This is magnificent." Alex took the doll, handling it carefully. He turned to Tessa as he examined its arm. "You were right, I've never seen anything like this before. I wonder who makes the plastic?"

Ana held out her hands for the doll. "Hans made the dolls, but I don't know where the plastic came from. Please give it back to me."

Alex handed the doll back carefully and Ana hugged it lovingly.

"Did Tessa tell you about the other one that was stolen?" she asked.

"Yes she did. You must keep this one safe. Are you sure you wouldn't like me to keep it for you?"

Ana hugged the doll even closer. "No, thank you, I will keep it. but please find Hans for me. I miss him so much."

Tessa put her arm round Ana and looked at Alex. "Is there anything you can do?"

"I'll certainly try," he said. "I'm beginning to get an idea. This plastic could be very important."

After a short conversation, Tessa and Alex took their leave of Ana, Tessa promising to be in touch the next day to take Ana to the exhibition."

In the car on the way back to the hotel Alex said, "I like your friend, but something is going on and we need to get to the bottom of it. Will you have dinner with me tonight so that we can talk this over?"

Tessa suddenly felt very guilty. "Sorry, Alex, I'm doing something else tonight, but don't forget we have a date on Saturday at the river."

"Yes, of course." Alex looked thoughtful.

It was nearly eight o'clock when Tessa returned to her room.

At about eight thirty, she had finished dressing, put her coat on and was about to go down, when the phone rang. It was Alex.

"I'm in the lobby. Can you come down? I've brought the exhibition pass for your friend."

Tessa felt a moment of panic. *I wish he would stop turning up unexpectedly. Serge will be there waiting for me. What should I do?*

As she came out of the lift Alex stepped forward.

"Here's the pass." He handed it to her. "I decided to see if I could change your mind about dinner."

She could see Serge standing some way off.

Thinking quickly, she took the pass and said, "Thanks for that, but I told you I had other plans for tonight." She turned, feeling terrible, and walked away from him towards Serge.

Alex watched as Tess put her arm in Serge's and walked out of the hotel.

Tessa felt tense, wondering what Alex would think and where Serge would take her.

"The café's not far," he said. "It's Italian, I know the owner, I often eat there."

They walked to a side road. "There it is," he said. The sign outside the café said *Die Turteltaube.*

"The turtledove." He led her into the brightly lit interior. They sat at a side table covered with a fresh linen tablecloth patterned with turtle doves.

Tessa looked around at the clientele, mainly a mixture of young couples. "This is nice," she said, "What should we eat?"

"I often have Zurcher Geschnetzeltes. It means Zurich sliced meat, but it's good. Try it." He turned to the waitress, "Hi, Lena, two Geschnetzeltes please and some red wine?" He looked inquiringly at Tessa who nodded.

"What have I let myself in for?" she asked with a laugh.

Serge looked solemn. "It's fine. Mainly thin sliced veal in a creamy sauce with onion and mushrooms."

When it came Tessa took one look. "What a plateful. I don't know if I can manage all this."

Serge laughed. "Just eat what you can, you'll like it."

The veal was beautifully tender, and Tessa enjoyed it, eating more than she had intended.

They toasted each other with red wine, and Serge told her that the wine was from Sicily. It was rough and warming and Tessa began to enjoy herself. Thoughts of Alex faded from her mind as they finished the meal with almond and chocolate cake doused in Strega.

Tessa leant back while Serge ordered coffee.

"Black for me," Tessa said, "That was a magnificent meal. Thank you for bringing me."

At that moment the chef appeared, shaking Serge's hand.

"Markus," Serge said. "Wonderful meal, as usual. May I introduce my friend, Tessa."

Markus, a large jolly man wearing an immaculate white apron wrapped around his ample stomach, bowed. "A pleasure to meet a friend of Serge's. You make a nice couple."

Tessa felt her cheeks going red. She turned away, coughing

to cover her embarrassment.

Serge escorted her back to the hotel and as they parted in the foyer, Tessa gave him a hug. "Thank you Serge, I really enjoyed that."

He looked nervously at her and then boldly gave her a tiny kiss on the cheek. "I hope we can meet again," he said.

"I'm sure we shall," Tessa said as he backed away, nearly falling over the potted palm near the entrance.

Tessa went up to her room feeling happy and relaxed.

So different from Alex and his sophistication, she thought, as she curled up in bed and went to sleep.

Tessa woke to lovely sunshine. She rolled out of bed and opened the window, looking down into the street below.

Friday was a working day for most people, hurrying, scurrying to work, babies being pushed in prams, street cleaners cleaning.

She drew a breath of the cold clear air, closed the window and went to the bathroom to wash.

At breakfast she saw the same motley collection of males in the dining room, but Tessa, in a good mood after her evening with Serge, looked benevolently on them.

As she sat having her usual breakfast, she reflected on the difference between Alex and Serge. Admittedly Serge was more her age, she thought. He was fun and the evening had gone well. Contrast that with Alex, who was obviously attracted to her. He was older, more experienced and sophisticated. They were both attractive in different ways. Serge boyish, eager, inexperienced in the ways of women, but fun. Alex, well hmm, she would see.

After breakfast she phoned Ana to say that she was on her way to pick her up.

This time, when she got in her taxi, there was no sign of Ted and Fred, so she assumed that they must have already gone to the exhibition hall.

She picked Ana up and they went on to the exhibition. Tessa wasn't going to any lectures, so she devoted her time to exploring the exhibitions with Ana.

Ana shielded her eyes as they walked into the hall. "It's so bright, with all these lights and the colours."

"You'll get used to it. It hit me the same way yesterday. Let's explore a bit before I show you the robots."

They wandered around looking at the various that were displaying all sorts of plastic kitchen equipment, knives, plates, spoons, plastic bags, bottles. They came at last to the Roboplastix stand, where the doll-like robots were still performing their tasks. Tessa looked round for Alex but saw no sign of him. Ana caught her arm. She was staring at a large man talking to one of the assistants.

"That's him," she said, gripping Tessa's arm.

"Ouch, you're hurting my arm Ana. What's wrong?"

"It's him, the man who stole my doll."

Tessa looked across. "You're right, it is him. What's he doing here?"

At that moment the man saw them standing there, and immediately turned and made for the back of the stand.

"What can we do? He's getting away." Ana was panicking.

"What's wrong?" Alex had come up behind them.

"That man." Ana pointed. "He's the one that stole my doll."

Alex looked at where she was pointing. "It can't be," he said. "That's Eric, my partner. Come on, I'll introduce you."

He went over to one of the assistants. "Where's Eric?"

"He was here a moment ago. I saw him go out the back."

Alex went to the back of the stand, calling, "Eric, Eric." He turned back. "He's gone. That was strange."

"It's him, I'm sure it is." Ana was shaking.

Tessa held on to her. "Yes, it was him. Alex, did you say he was your partner?"

"Yes, but are you sure it was your burglar?"

"It was him, we can't both be wrong."

Alex looked thoughtful. "This is the first time I've seen him after I got back from England, I think he's been avoiding me. I wonder why. I'll see if I can get hold of him. He can't have gone far. Why don't you two go and have a coffee? I'll come as soon as I've located him, see what he knows about this."

Ana tugged at Tessa. "I think I want to go home," she said, still looking frightened.

"I'll take her back, Alex. If you get any news, give me a ring, you've got my mobile number." Tessa held Ana's hand.

"Yes, fine. How about dinner tonight, if you're free?"

"I must have dinner with Ana tonight. She needs my company."

"Okay, I'll phone if I get news." Alex sounded disappointed.

"Don't forget our date at the pier tomorrow, ten sharp."

"I'll be there, don't worry, and if I get any news today, I'll phone."

Tessa hastened Ana out of the exhibition hall into a taxi and took her home.

CHAPTER FOUR

Back at her apartment, Ana apologised.
"I'm sorry, that was the man, and when I saw him it brought it all back."

Tessa tried to reassure her. "Don't worry, I'm sure Alex will sort it out. Would you like me to stay with you?"

"No, I'll be fine. This is my day off, so I've got some domestic chores to do. Would you like to come to dinner?"

"That would be lovely but why don't I take you out? Serge showed me a good café. *The Turtle Dove*."

"Oh, I know it," Ana clapped her hands. "Yes, let's go there."

"I'll come for you at about eight. Are you sure you'll be all right till then?"

"I'll be fine. Let me know if there's any news?" Ana smiled, sounding more like her usual self.

"Of course, see you later."

Tessa went back to the hotel and spent the afternoon writing up a report for her Head of Department. As she finished, she turned to Bella, her doll, sitting patiently on the bed.

"Why would Alex's partner want to steal Ana's dolls? No one steals dolls. It must be the plastic." She ran her hand over Bella's golden locks. Then she clapped her hand to her own head. "I'm an idiot. Of course, it's the plastic, but how did Alex's partner know about the dolls unless Hans told him? He stole them to analyse the plastic, and since Alex is his partner he must be involved."

The phone rang. It was Alex.

"My partner Eric Weber seems to have vanished. He hasn't been seen since Ana saw him at the exhibition. He's not at headquarters, but he may have gone to our research centre. There's something strange there as well—we've lost all communication with the Centre, no phones and no reaching them by radio. They have a powerful radio transmitter, but even that doesn't seem to be working."

Tessa could tell from his voice that he was worried, but she decided not to worry him further by accusing him of being involved.

He continued, "I ought to go to our research centre, but I've promised you I will go to the plastics demonstration tomorrow."

She could tell that he hoped she would release him from his promise, but she had no intention in doing so.

"Yes, you must come, but I could come with you afterwards. I'd like to see your research centre."

Alex laughed, "I'm not sure you would want to come."

"Why not?"

"It's on a mountain."

Tessa remembered what she had been told at the exhibition, a research centre at the top of a mountain. "Sounds great. The demonstration on the river should finish by lunchtime tomorrow. Could we go up in the afternoon? How do you get there?"

"There is a train that goes up the mountain, but we do it the easy way, by helicopter."

Tessa felt a surge of excitement. " I've never been in one. Two adventures in one day, fantastic."

"Right, I'll lay on the helicopter to take us."

"I would enjoy that very much. So, see you tomorrow at the pier." She set the phone down.

Smoothing Bella's hair, she picked her doll up and gave it

a hug. "No one's going to steal you, so don't worry. I must go down for tea. See you soon."

She went down to the lounge, taking her book with her. She had tea and then read until it was time to go to pick Ana up for dinner.

Ana was waiting for her and, as before, the meal at the Turtledove was a great success, the proprietor recognising her from her previous visit with Serge.

After dinner, she left Ana at her apartment agreeing that Ana could fix her dinner the next night.

As she lay in bed, her doll on the pillow next to her, she thought sleepily about how Alex would respond to the plastics demonstration.

Next morning at breakfast she looked at her watch. *Heavens, I'm supposed to be there for ten o'clock. It's almost nine thirty now.* She rose hurriedly from the breakfast table.

Already dressed in blouse and slacks, she went back to her room, slipped on a sweater and her coat, took a quick look in the mirror, picked up her shoulder bag, and went down the stairs past the pictures, their gaze seeming to follow her. The concierge called a taxi, and she was off. She walked along the pier, past what were obviously pleasure boats, until she saw Ted and Fred waving at her from a very powerful looking boat. As she approached, she could see the name *Friends of Fish* painted on its bows.

Already a small crowd of reporters and cameramen were assembled on the rear boat deck, a pile of plastic waste piled up at the very back.

"Welcome," Fred called as she walked up the narrow gangplank and onto the boat deck. "Your friend is already here." He pointed to Alex, who was standing in the bows looking at the pile of waste.

"We're just waiting for two other people, and then we are off," Fred said.

Tessa walked over to Alex, drawing her coat closer as the wind whipped across the deck. "Good morning," she said cheerily.

"You think so?" Alex looked up, obviously in a grumpy mood. He was dressed in a windcheater and slacks. "You chose a cold morning for this part of our adventure. The river will be even colder." He shivered, looked down at the water swirling in an oily way below them. "I've only come because you persuaded me. I hope it's worth it."

"Of course it's worth it. You'll feel better once we get going, but" — she looked closely at him — "It isn't just the river, is it? Something else is wrong. What is it?"

Alex rubbed his hands together, obviously trying to get warm. "Stop reading my mind. Yes, there is something else wrong. Eric seems to have vanished like your precious Hans. He must be up at our research centre, and as I can't get in touch with them I must get up there as soon as I can."

"Cheer up Alex, we'll go up to your mountain hideaway straight after this demonstration. I want you to see what happens when plastic pollutes our rivers and oceans."

"I know that already," he said impatiently. "I thought this was an exercise in cleaning it up?" He glanced over the pile of waste.

"You may think you know," Tessa clung on to the side as the gangplank was taken away and the boat began to move, "but it's different when you see it for real."

They stepped back as a group of people came up to them. Fred, wearing a yachting cap, stood at the front with two other men standing on either side of the pile of plastic waste, waiting.

"I want to explain," he said, nodding at the pile of plastic. "For our demonstration today, we have been allowed to bring our own waste. The River Limmat is virtually waste and pollution free, thanks to the efforts of the City Council, so we are going to have to dirty it up a bit."

That raised a laugh as the boat was manoeuvred into midstream a little way from the pier.

"We were given permission to use this stretch of water," Fred said. " Farther down, river bathing is allowed, and as the water flows this way, we are not interfering with the bathers at all. Not that there will be many on a cold day like this."

Tessa pulled her coat tighter, noticing that a number of small pleasure boats were coming up the river and passing them. One stopped and nosed closer, people on deck watching what was happening.

"That's what we should be doing," she said to Alex as the other craft sailed by.

"Boating on the river? Well, I do have a small yacht. I'll take you out in it sometime."

The two men slid the protective rail back from the side of the boat, lifted the tarpaulin containing the waste, and threw it in the water. Alex leant forward to watch.

Tessa thought he was leaning too far over now that the rail had been removed and without thinking she grabbed him. "You had better stand back. We don't want you falling in."

He turned and grinned. "Falling in that cold water would be a bit disastrous." He moved back.

The mass of plastic bottles and other debris floated on the surface of the water.

"Now lower the collar quickly," Fred commanded the two men. "We don't want it to get away from us."

The men quickly caught hold of a plastic apron with a flotation collar attached to it, dropping it over the side with an almighty splash. Once it was in the water, Tessa could see how it would work. The boat came about, moving the floating collar round the waste, enclosing it. As it did so, the reporters and cameramen surged forward to get good shots of the collar floating in the water.

Although Alex had moved back, Tessa was still standing quite close to the edge, and in the rush she was pushed forward. She felt herself losing her balance. One of the reporters tried to grab her by the coat, but his hand slipped. He grabbed her shoulder bag, and she fell into the water with a tremendous splash. As she fell, the thought ran through her mind that she ought to have been wearing a life jacket.

The water was icy cold. She went under, her coat holding her down until at last, after what seemed an age, she fought her way to the surface. She could hear the cries of concern from the pleasure boat.

Normally she was a strong swimmer, but her coat was impeding progress. As she struggled to free herself from it, she heard another splash. She turned, treading water. It was Alex.

"Did you fall in as well?" she asked, spluttering, as he surfaced beside her.

Alex trod water. "No, I dived in to save you. Can you swim?"

"Of course, but I must get out of this coat, it's dragging me down."

Alex struggled, helping to get it off her shoulders.

Freed from the coat, which floated away, Tessa started away from him with a breaststroke. "Come on," she called back. "We must get out quickly or die of hypothermia."

"I'm with you." He followed her with a strong overarm stroke.

Tessa could still feel her sodden clothes threatening to drag her down.

They reached the bank. Alex grabbed her round the waist, helping her out as spectators bent down and pulled them both to safety.

As they lay for a moment panting on the edge, an elderly woman came forward followed by her husband. "Come to my house. You must get out of your wet clothes as soon as possible. It's just along here." She pointed to one of the small houses just back from the riverbank.

Tessa's teeth were chattering. "Thank you," she said. "Come on, Alex."

Alex helped her up and they set off.

Tessa's clothes were dripping with water and her feet felt like blocks of ice. She cast a glance at Alex. He looked like a drowned rat. His brown hair was plastered over his face and his clothes hung loose on him.

The sympathetic crowd quickly parted, allowing them to follow the woman.

It was a small house but, as they squelched over the threshold, Tessa could feel the immediate change in temperature. It hit her like a warm, wet blanket.

The woman turned to Alex. "You must wait down here. My husband Jakob will look after you."

She took Tessa by the hand and led her up to the bathroom. Closing the door firmly she helped her undress, then giving her a large towel to dry herself, went and fetched a skirt and jumper.

"They're probably a bit big for you," she said with a smile. "I was about your size when I was younger, but" — she spread her arms out — "I've expanded a bit since then."

"You're very kind." Tessa began to feel warmer, but her teeth were still chattering."

When she was dressed, they went downstairs to find Alex clad in a golfing jacket and trousers that flapped round his ankles. He was standing by a glowing fire warming his hands.

When Tessa saw him she burst into laughter.

"What are you laughing at?" Alex looked uncomfortable.

"No, nothing." Tessa put her hand up to her face.

The woman was also smiling. "I should have introduced myself properly, I'm Lina, and this is my husband Jakob." She put her arm round her husband's waist.

"I'm Tessa, and this is Alex, a friend of mine," Tessa said, moving closer to the fire.

"A brave friend, I think," Lina said. "You were both lucky to get out of the water so quickly. We saw what happened."

Alex was beginning to revive. "Thank you both for saving us. Could you call a taxi? We must go back."

"Won't you stay to get properly warm?" Lina asked.

"No, we must get back, our friends will be worrying about us, but thank you so much for rescuing us."

"I will call a taxi," Jakob left the room to telephone.

Tessa, being more practical than Alex, said to Lina, "I'll get the clothes you lent us laundered and sent back to you as soon as we can."

"Thank you my dear. Here are your own clothes." Lina handed Tessa a large bag.

"You had better take this, Alex, it's too heavy for me," Tessa staggered under its weight.

"Here are your shoes," Lina said, handing them to her. "They're still a little damp, although Jacob has tried to dry them for you."

Jakob came back into the room. "Taxi in five minutes," he said. "In the meantime, stay by the fire and keep warm."

The taxi arrived, honking its horn.

"Thank you both," Tessa said. "You are angels."

Jakob looked at his wife. "Now that the children are grown up and left home we don't get many opportunities . . ."

Lina hugged him close, then kissed Tessa on both cheeks. "Bless you both, you make a nice couple."

Tessa felt embarrassed, "Come on Alex, we must go."

As they got into the taxi, Alex gave directions to the driver. Tessa heard the word chateau.

They waved goodbye. Tessa looked from the taxi to the river, but the boat had gone.

"They must have finished the demonstration," Alex said.

"Well, that was a very convincing demonstration of how to fall in the water. Rather than go back to find the boat, you must come back with me to my chateau. A nice warm bath is what you need."

"Sounds wonderful," Tessa said, conscious that her teeth were still chattering.

Alex sank back in his seat. "Do you think we should have tipped them? They were so kind."

"A nice thought," Tessa said, "but that's the sort of help money can't buy."

"Well, I could send them some chocolates when we return their clothes."

Tessa looked across at Alex sitting there looking like a lost boy, hair plastered back, wriggling uncomfortably in his too-large jacket.

Maybe I'm wrong about this man, perhaps he isn't involved in the theft of the doll. He seems kind and honest. He did jump in the water to try to save me, and now he wants to show his appreciation for the help they gave us.

The taxi turned into a winding drive and drove up to the house, a chateau built in the French style. Alex handed Tessa out, paid the driver, and with his arm round her waist, ushered her into the warmth of the front hall, where they were met by a grey-haired man almost standing at attention as Alex greeted him.

"Jules, this is Miss Corston. Will you ask Emma to prepare a bath for her? The Royal Suite, I think."

Jules very slightly raised his eyebrows.

Alex caught the look and laughed. He turned to Tessa. "Jules is old fashioned but a good butler." Then said to Jules, "Miss Corston and I fell in the river. It's a long story, but she needs a warm bath as soon as possible."

"I will attend to it immediately." Jules bowed slightly, then went rapidly up the magnificent staircase.

"Come on up. The Royal Suite has a bedroom and sitting

room as well as a terrific bathroom. You will also find clothes there. I keep a selection of things for when guests are here."

No wonder Jules raised his eyebrows, Tessa thought, following Alex up the stairs.

The Royal Suite was magnificent. A four-poster bed dominated the bedroom. The bathroom led off through a door on the right, through which she could hear sounds of running water. The sounds stopped and a maid came out, gave a curtsey and left Tessa and Alex alone in the bedroom.

"It's all yours," Alex said. "I will leave you now and have a bath myself."

"Won't you want to use this bathroom?"

Alex smiled. "The chateau has three bathrooms so don't worry. I will see you later."

He turned and walked out into the corridor.

Tessa looked around. The room was decorated with magnificent wall hangings. She went into the bathroom to find a large bath filled with foaming water. Large fluffy bath towels hung nearby. She felt the temperature of the water. It was just right, so stripping off her borrowed clothes she stepped in. As she lay down, the gloriously warm water enveloped her body.

After the shock of the fall into the cold water of the River Limmat this bath was glorious. She was conscious of staying in it for too long when the bathroom door opened and Alex stood there clad only in a bathrobe.

Tessa found herself quivering as she looked at the powerful figure standing by the side of the bath.

"I know you would like to stay there," he said, covering his eyes, "but you really ought to come out. Let me help you."

He held up one of the large bath towels.

"Come on out. I won't look." He turned his back, holding out the towel.

Tessa rose naked from the bath, grabbed the towel and

pressed it to herself as she stepped out.

As she did so, Alex turned and caught her round the waist. The towel slipped and she was naked in front of him. He pulled her to him as she put up her hands and tried to push him away.

"I'm all wet," she protested laughing.

"Dry yourself against my bathrobe." He drew her closer as she felt the rough cloth against her breasts.

Her hands went down to the belt of his robe, undoing it so that his robe fell open to reveal his muscular body.

"You are wet," he said. "Let me dry you." He took the towel from where it had fallen and began to rub her gently all over.

Tessa quivered, reaching up and tearing the robe from his body.

"There, now you are dry." He threw the towel away, their bodies met as he pulled her to him.

Seemingly without effort he lifted her and carried her into the bedroom, placing her gently on the soft sheets.

She knew that she wanted this man, but should she let him take her like this? It seemed so natural, and when he bent over her, with his hands caressing her body, she knew that this was right. She reached up and pulled his head down to hers. As their lips met, Tessa felt her whole body melt into his.

Still pressing his lips on hers, he lifted his hands to her breasts, caressing her nipples as she wriggled under his touch.

He stroked her body, reaching lower towards her moist centre. Suddenly he stopped, his body stiffening as though in shock. He pulled away from her.

"No, this isn't right, it's not fair on you." He jumped up and backed quickly out of the room.

Tessa was so aroused that his withdrawal came as a tremendous shock to her system. She lay there, turning her head into the pillow with great racking sobs.

Her sobs turned to anger. *How dare he do this to me.*

She lay there for a while, her thoughts in a whirl, then flinging herself off the bed she began to explore the room in an effort to calm down. Although naked she walked over and opened drawers in the cabinets.

To her surprise she found a selection of clean women's underwear carefully packed between layers of fragrantly smelling tissue paper.

So this is where he keeps his women.

Tessa took out a dainty pair of panties and tried them on. Bras of various sizes filled the next drawer. Tessa laughed at the huge size of one of them, then selected one her size. Next she opened the wardrobe, and sure enough it was filled with a selection of dresses. She held up a gorgeous cream dress in front of her and looked in the full-length mirror. She nodded approvingly and put it on.

Now for shoes. Her own were still slightly damp, but in the bottom of the wardrobe she found a shoe rack and selected a pair of sandals that fitted perfectly.

Feeling a little calmer, she stood for a moment by the window looking out onto immaculate lawns. The feeling of rage left her and she began to think more clearly.

I must get out of here. How can I get out without him seeing me?

As she was thinking this, the bedroom door opened and Alex, fully dressed in a shirt and slacks, stood in the opening.

For a moment no words were said. Then Alex spoke, as though nothing had happened "I think we're going to have to postpone our trip up the mountain. We could arrange it for tomorrow."

Her words choked in her throat. "Oh Alex." She looked up at him as he put his arms around her.

"I'm sorry I got carried away. You are so beautiful and precious to me." He caressed her hair as she nestled into his chest. Then he gently eased her away. "I must get Stephan to run you back to your hotel. How about coming back to my place for lunch tomorrow?" Holding her hand he said, "I look forward to seeing you. Come as soon as you can. I'll fix lunch for one o'clock and have the helicopter standing by to take us up the mountain afterwards. Don't worry about your wet clothes. I'll arrange for them to be laundered."

Tessa felt a sudden surge of love. She raised her hand to his face and stroked it lightly.

Down in the hall, he put a man's coat around her shoulders and kissed her gently. He handed her into the Daimler that was waiting outside the front door, and waved goodbye.

Tessa lay back in the comfortable car seat, her mind going over recent events.

What strange behaviour. I wanted him to take me. Why did he suddenly break away?

She could find no logical explanation. The car drew up in front of the hotel. She stepped out and went into the hotel.

She reached the reception desk and asked for her key, and was handed it together with an envelope.

Making her way up to her room, she took off the borrowed clothes she was wearing, then, slipping on the fluffy bathrobe she sat on the bed next to Bella, her doll, and opened the letter. It was from Ted and Fred.

Dear Tessa,

What a terrible thing to happen. We watched as you both got out of the water and saw how you were helped by some of the crowd. We couldn't leave the boat to see if you were all right but if you are reading this we know you must be. Please accept our apologies for what happened and to make amends could we invite you to have dinner with us this evening at say, eight o'clock and we can give you your shoulder bag back?

Yours, Ted Clapton and Fred Jackson

Tessa folded the note slowly and put it on the table. She turned to Bella. "Now what do I do? I promised Ana I would spend the evening with her."

Bella stared back impassively. Tessa picked her up and gave her a hug.

I know. She put the doll back on the bed. *Why not invite Ana to join us? We can make a foursome.* She picked up the phone and asked reception if they could put her through to either Mr Clapton or Mr Jackson.

Reception told her that Mr Clapton wasn't answering his phone but put her through to Mr Jackson. She heard Fred's voice.

"Is that Fred?" she said, sitting down on the bed. "Thank you for your note. I'd love to dine with you tonight."

"Good," Fred said. "We felt terrible about what happened. The crowd shouldn't have pushed forwards like that, but we saw you being rescued. Are you all right?"

"A bit shaken but no permanent damage. The water was very cold though, we were fortunate to get out so quickly."

"Thank goodness, well come and have a meal with us to-night."

Tessa could hear the genuine concern in Fred's voice. "There's just one thing. I had actually promised to see a friend of mine tonight. Her name is Ana. Rather than disappoint her, would you mind if I brought her along?"

Fred laughed, a ringing genuine laugh. "That makes it like a blind date," he said. "By all means bring her along. Ted and I are just so pleased you're none the worse for your adventure. Meet you at eight in the dining room."

Tessa put the phone down, looked up Ana's number, and phoned her.

"Ana, I know I said I would come over tonight, but I've had rather a shock to my system and we've both been invited to dine at my hotel by two men I met at the conference. If you'll come, I will explain when I see you."

Ana sounded a bit uncertain, but she said, "Yes, I'll come,

but who are these two strange men?"

"I think you'll like them. They're from England. Very respectable. I '11explain properly when I see you. Come to my room around seven."

"Yes, I will. See you then."

After her shower, Tessa turned again to the report she was writing. *Now I've really got something to report – writing an account of my adventure with the plastic waste.*

Time seemed to fly by, and soon Ana arrived just after seven. "Sorry I'm late," she said, flopping down onto a chair. "The traffic was terrible."

She took off her coat and was dressed in a simple calf length silk dress with three-quarter length sleeves, a coloured belt around her tiny waist.

"You look gorgeous," Tessa said admiringly. "Both men are bound to fall for you."

"I don't want that to happen. I want my Hans." Ana pouted.

"Don't worry. I was just joking – I'm sure they're both married. I expect they'll show us pictures of their children before the evening is out."

Ana sat on the edge of the bed. "How did you come to meet them?"

"It's a long story, but briefly I met them manning one of the exhibits at the conference. They invited me to a demonstration on the river." Tessa laughed. "And I fell in."

"Oh, no." Ana looked concerned. "The river water is so cold at this time of year. Are you all right?"

"I swam to the shore and got helped by a kindly couple. Oh, and I forgot. I had Alex Baxter with me."

"Alex Baxter, the new boyfriend?" Ana leant forward expectantly.

Tessa smiled. "Perhaps, but I told you it was a long story. The important thing is, the two men in charge of the demonstration, Ted and Fred, felt guilty about me falling in and so asked me to dinner, and when I told them I had promised to be with you this evening, they invited you along as well. I'll explain about Alex some other time."

Tessa put the finishing touches to her makeup, dressed in her elegant blue dress, and they went down at eight o'clock and found Ted and Fred waiting for them.

Tessa introduced Ana to the two men, and as they sat down at the table, Fred again apologised to Tessa about the accident. "It was the reporters who were at fault, pushing to the front like that. You were lucky not to get trampled in the rush even before you were pushed in."

Tessa turned to Ana. "It was quite frightening. I was forced forward, lost my balance, and fell into the water."

"Who was the brave fellow who jumped in to save you?" Ted asked.

"Foolish fellow, you mean." Tessa smiled. "That was Alex Baxter, the Head of Roboplastix Inc. The firm I asked you about the other day."

"What was he doing on our boat?" Fred asked.

Tessa giggled. "I thought it would be a good idea to show him what happened to plastics when they pollute our rivers, making him more aware of the problem, and he did land right in it didn't he?"

"He did indeed." Fred laughed with her.

After the meal they took their coffee in the dining room, Ted and Fred telling them stories of what they considered to be their ill-spent youth which Tessa privately thought were rather boring, although she liked both of them. She was tempted to tell them some of her stories, but decided that her tomboy adventures wouldn't be appropriate. Instead, she encouraged Ana to talk about the Alpine holidays and skiing that they had enjoyed together.

It was getting late, and Tessa stifled a yawn.

"Thank you both for a lovely evening," she said. "I think we ought to go. Especially as Ana has to drive back."

"We enjoyed it," Ted said, "and thank goodness you are all right. Next time we do a river demonstration, we shall make sure everyone is wearing a life jacket."

Tessa and Ana said goodnight, leaving the two men in the bar.

Tessa waved Ana off and was going wearily to bed when the receptionist called, "Miss Corston, I have a message for you." He handed her a folded paper.

On it there was a short message.

You were out when I phoned. Don't forget lunch tomorrow, one o'clock at my chateau, and then we go on to the research centre by helicopter.

Alex.

On Sunday morning she woke with a pleasant feeling of anticipation.

She rang Ana, just to keep in touch. "I enjoyed last night. Nice couple of men. What did you think?"

"Yes, great," Ana said. "I think Fred had his eye on you."

Tessa could feel herself blushing. "Nonsense, you were the prettiest of the two of us. How are you going to spend your day?"

"As it's Sunday, I'm going to do some domestic chores, and Serge is coming to tea this afternoon."

"Still no news of Hans I suppose?"

"No, the police still haven't contacted me."

Tessa could tell by the way Ana's voice fell that she was still worrying. "Well, I'm off to lunch at Alex's chateau. I hope he might have some news for us about your sweetheart, and I've been promised a helicopter trip up a mountain in the afternoon."

"Lunch with Alex, and helicopters. You do get around."

Tessa could tell from Ana's tone that she was teasing her. She rang off, promising to tell Ana all about the lunch and the trip.

After breakfast she went back to her room and surveyed her limited wardrobe.

What's suitable for lunch at a chateau? I wish I had brought more clothes with me.

In the end she decided on slacks and a blouse. She hoped that with his being a man, he wouldn't remember that was what she had worn on their first evening together.

She had Alex's coat, but that must be returned. What was she to do?

Fortunately the Hotel Splendide lived up to its reputation. A call to the deputy manager resulted in the arrival of an assistant from a nearby dress shop bringing several coats, of which Tessa chose the warmest, paying with her credit card.

When the man had gone, she put on the coat, looked at the address Alex had given her, and phoned down for a taxi.

The taxi went up the winding drive to the house. She walked up the short flight of steps as the door opened and Alex welcomed her in.

"Come on through." Alex took her coat, and after she handed him the one he had lent her he hung them both in an alcove to the left of the stairs.

"We're lunching on the terrace," he said. "Let me lead the way." He glanced admiringly at her but made no comment.

They walked through a large airy room with a high decorated ceiling and ornate chairs stationed round the walls.

"This used to be the ballroom in the old days," Alex said. "We use it occasionally when the firm is giving a reception."

He led her out through French doors onto a large terrace overlooking the garden. A table was set with white linen and sparkling tableware.

"Would you like a drink first?" he asked, holding a chair

for her.

As she sat down, Tessa felt overwhelmed by the magnificence of the setting. Beyond the stone balustrade, the formal garden stretched out across a lawn to a copse of trees. Everything was trimmed and neat.

"What I would really like," she said, breathing in the fresh clear air, "is a walk in your garden before lunch."

"Of course, let me get your coat." He went back into the house and came back with Tessa's coat, having put on a jacket himself.

He took her hand, leading her down a short flight of steps into the garden. "We can make it a circular walk if we go down by the stream."

The garden was superb. They walked down through a lightly wooded area to a cluster of trees, leaves crunching under their feet.

As they walked, Alex talked about their experience with the plastic waste demonstration. When it came to the part where he had jumped in to rescue Tessa, they both laughed, and he gently put his arm round her.

They came to the stream, water gurgling over small boulders, and as Alex's arm tightened around her waist, she thought he was going to kiss her. A pleasant feeling flooded through her body. She half turned towards him.

As he pulled her close there was an interruption.

A small boy raced up the path and flung his arms round Alex's legs.

"Daddy, daddy," he cried, "You promised to play with me this morning, but you're with this lady."

Alex drew back. His arm dropped from around Tessa's waist. He patted the boy on the head. "I can play with you later this afternoon," he said. "Tessa, this is Luka."

Tessa swung away in shock. "You're married," she said, trembling.

"It's a long story." Alex looked alarmed as a young woman appeared on the path calling, "Luka, Luka, where are you?"

One look was enough for Tessa. Bristling with anger, she looked from the boy to the young woman. She turned abruptly and said, "Goodbye Alex, I don't think I will stay for lunch or the helicopter trip after all."

Hampered by the boy with his arms round Alex's legs, he said, "No, wait. Tessa!"

But she was gone.

Tessa walked rapidly back to the house, through the ballroom and out into the hall.

Disoriented for a moment, she ran to the front door, opened it and went quickly down the steps and onto the drive. As she ran down the drive she thought she heard Alex calling behind her, but she kept running.

Out on the main road a taxi came up to her and she signalled frantically for it to stop. It went past and then drew up with a jerk. She ran to it and jumped in just as it began to rain.

"Where do you want to go?" the driver asked.

She thought quickly — should she go back to the hotel? She felt the need to talk to someone, as she could still feel the shock of Alex's treachery, so she gave the driver the address of Ana's apartment.

Ana opened the door to her. "Tessa, you look terrible. What's happened? Come in, come in."

Tessa, drenched and feeling like a train wreck, stumbled into the apartment.

CHAPTER FIVE

Ana, thunderstruck, took one look at her. "What's wrong? No, let me take your coat, then sit down, tell me all about it." Ana looked concerned. "Wait, I'll make some tea, or do you need something stronger?"

"Tea would be nice," Tessa said. "I'm dripping wet all over your floor. Can I use your bathroom to freshen up, then I'll explain."

Ana waved in the direction of the bathroom. "Feel free. I'll have tea waiting for you when you come back."

As Tessa headed for the bathroom, the doorbell rang.

"That will be Serge. He said he would come over this afternoon." Ana ran to the door. "Hi, come on in."

Serge shook off his heavy jacket. "It's raining out there. I'm going to get your floor all wet." He shook his coat outside.

"You're the second person to worry about that. Here, let me take it."

She took the jacket into the kitchen. Serge followed her.

"Hang it up over here." She handed him a coat hanger and pointed to the clothes rack on one side of the room.

"Who is the second person?" he asked.

"Tessa's just come. I'm going to make tea for both of you. Go and sit down while I make it. I've got some ginger cake."

Serge went obediently into the other room as Tessa emerged from the bathroom. Hair combed, colour coming back into her cheeks, she looked more like herself.

"Serge," she said, as he rose to greet her. She gave him a hug.

Ana came in with the tea tray. "Sit down, both of you." She busied herself pouring the tea and offering cake. She looked questioningly at Tessa.

Tessa sipped her tea. "I don't want to talk about it at the moment." She glanced at Serge.

Serge caught the glance and looked down at his plate.

Looking contrite, Tessa said, "It's nothing really, Serge. It's, well, I feel a bit washed out after my adventure falling into the water."

"What!" Serge looked at her with concern.

"You haven't told Serge about that." Ana glanced at Serge. "Did you know?"

"No, it's the first I've heard about it." Serge looked shocked. "What happened? Tell us about it."

Tessa began describing her meeting with Ted and Fred and their invitation to watch the plastic waste demonstration on the river ending up with her being pushed in the water and having to swim to the bank.

"I was rescued by a nice couple who took me to their house and dried me out. I must remember to return the clothes they lent me." As she spoke she was conscious that she had edited Alex out of the picture.

"That's terrible," Serge said. "You could easily have got hypothermia in such cold water. The river is not a place to bathe in at this time of year."

"It was fortunate that this friendly couple helped me, otherwise it might have been worse."

"What an awful thing to happen." Serge glanced up at Tessa. "I'm glad you were rescued so quickly."

"You do look all in. Has the conference finished now?" Ana asked.

"It's the last day today, but I'm not going. I've had enough of plastics for a while." Tessa mentally substituted the word *Alex* for *plastics*.

Ana looked carefully at her. "What you need is a few days' rest. I know! I've got a week's leave owing. How about going on one of our trips?"

Tessa sank back in her chair. "That sounds great. Probably just what I need." The memory of Alex, his son and young wife welled up in front of her.

"I would like to get out of Zurich for a bit."

"Right, let's plan it straight away." Ana sounded excited.

"Don't leave me out—I can drive you. Where would you like to go?" Serge asked.

"How about Bern for a few days?" Ana suggested.

Tessa considered for a moment. "Yes, we went there on one of our trips years ago. It would be great to go there again."

"How far is it?" Serge asked. "Not that it matters. I'll drive you there anyway."

"That's nice of you, Serge, but I think it would be better if Ana and I go by train."

"Rubbish," Serge said. "A nice drive is exactly what you need. I won't be able to stay, though, as I'll have to come back in case we hear from Hans."

Ana looked troubled at the mention of Hans.

"Don't worry," Serge reassured her. "As long as I know where you are, if I get any news, I'll phone. So you'll let me drive you?"

"It's very good of you, Serge, are you sure?" Tessa remembered his driving from the last time.

"No problem," he said, eyeing the last piece of cake on the tray.

"That's settled then." Ana put the teacups and plates on the tray. "Eat this last piece, Serge, otherwise it will go to waste."

Serge took the cake almost in one mouthful, handing Ana his plate. "When shall we go?" he asked.

"The sooner the better for me," Tessa said.

Ana thought for a moment. "Let's go tomorrow. I'll phone

up my manager. I know it's Sunday, but I've got his home number. He'll be a bit surprised, but he's a good sort. He knows I've got leave coming, so I'm sure he won't mind."

"Shall we book into the hotel where we stayed before?" Tessa asked. "Can you remember its name?"

"I'll look it up. What was it, two years ago? Hang on while I look in my old diary. I think it was the Hotel Wiltshire." She went to the bureau drawer and hunted among the papers, triumphantly holding up her diary. She went through it. "Here it is, Hotel Wiltshire, I was right."

"Good, I'll phone and book when I get back to the hotel." Tessa was anxious for action that would make her feel better.

It was agreed to meet tomorrow. Serge would pick Tessa up at the hotel first, then go round to Ana's place, and they would go on to Bern for a three-day holiday.

Serge drove Tessa back to her hotel at his usual breakneck speed.

"I'm surprised you don't get a ticket," she said, as he deposited her at the hotel entrance."

"Swiss driving laws are very strict," he said. "Traffic fines can be pretty heavy. It may look fast to you, but I'm very careful to obey the laws. For example, you may have noticed the warning triangle on the back seat. You're not allowed to put it in the boot, it has to be easily got at in case of a breakdown. There are all sorts of rules like that."

Tessa laughed nervously. "You must be a very good driver, but it does seem fast."

Serge grinned. "See you tomorrow," he waved, and was off.

As Tessa returned to her room, Alex and his treachery returned to her mind. She picked up her doll, Bella, and hugged her. Then holding it close she said, "I thought that was the beginning of a beautiful friendship, but it turns out he's just like every other man. You and Ana are my true friends."

She put Bella carefully down on the bed. "Now before I do anything else, I must phone the hotel in Bern."

The receptionist at the Hotel Wiltshire answered the phone almost immediately. Yes, there were two rooms available for three days starting the next day. She was fortunate, as there had just been a cancellation. Otherwise the hotel was full, and they would only have been able to give her one room.

Tessa rang Ana straight away to tell her the good news.

"See you tomorrow," Ana said. "I'll ring Serge and let him know."

As soon as Tessa put the phone down, Alex returned to her mind.

How could he do such a thing? Married with a young child, and who was the young woman? His wife? I seem to attract unsuitable men.

She sat on the bed stamping her feet. Her whole being raged against him. *What did he think he was doing? Just when I had begun to believe in him and love him.*

For the second time in her life, she had been let down by a man.

This was still in her mind as she walked down the stairs to dinner. She peered down nervously to the entrance hall as though expecting Alex to be waiting there with a bunch of flowers but there was no sign of him.

To her surprise, she felt a pang of disappointment. Her anger cooled. There must surely be some sort of explanation for the situation.

Men. Who needs them? On my own again. At least Ana is a good friend, and we shall enjoy our Bern trip.

Walking into the dining room, she met Ted and Fred just going to their table.

"Come and join us," Fred said. "We're off back to England tomorrow, so let's celebrate."

"Thanks, I will," Tessa smiled. At least these two men were good to know and didn't pose a threat.

It was a jolly meal, and because of the way she felt, Tessa drank a little too much wine.

After the meal she felt a little woozy.

She caught a glance between Fred and Ted. "I think I'll escort our guest to her room. I won't be long. See you back in the bar." Fred took her arm.

"It's been good to meet you," he said as they arrived at her door. "Both Ted and I have really enjoyed your company. You must look us up when you're back. Here's my card." He fished around in his wallet and took out a card giving the name of his company. Even in her slightly unfocussed state she saw that he was named as a senior executive.

As he handed it to her, he said, "Of course, if we manage to get a contract with your five-nation project, we shall probably be seeing more of you anyway."

"Not, I hope, to be pushed in the water again." Tessa laughed.

"We would be careful not to," he said, smiling.

Tessa shook hands with him. "Thanks for a lovely evening. It really took me out of myself. Good night."

Fred looked puzzled by her remark, but said, "Good night, sleep well."

Tessa closed her door and sank down onto the bed trying to analyse her feelings. She shook her head. *I'm too tired tonight, and we're going away in the morning.*

She got undressed quickly, gave Bella a hug, fell into bed, and was soon in a dreamless sleep.

Next morning she woke with a slight headache, had a hurried breakfast, and went back to her room to pack. Just as she was finishing, the phone rang. It was Serge calling from the entrance hall, where he was waiting to collect her.

He loaded her suitcase into the boot of his car, and they drove to Ana's apartment. Ana was waiting with two small cases which Serge also put into the boot, and they were off.

"I've looked up Bern," Serge said as they drew away from the kerb. "It's only about an hour and a half drive, so sit back and enjoy the ride."

Tessa and Ana sat in the back so they could talk, leaving Serge in the front to concentrate on his driving.

As they left the suburbs of Zurich, they passed under bridges and then they were out on the motorway. Traffic was fairly heavy, but contrary to Tessa's expectations, Serge drove carefully and not in the madcap way he had driven her previously.

"This is the A one motorway," he said, glancing back. "Are you both okay?"

"Yes, fine," Tessa said, smiling at Ana.

As they drove on, Tessa was surprised at how flat the landscape was. "I thought we would be winding through the mountains," she said, peering out of the window.

"No," Serge called back. "Bern is on a flat plateau, it's just hills and forests."

As they approached Bern, Serge stopped in a lay-by, setting his satnav to direct him to the Hotel Wiltshire.

The hotel was in the older part of Bern. Serge deposited them at the entrance.

"Do you want me to come in with you?" he asked.

"No, you ought to get back in case there is any word of Hans, "Ana said as a porter came out to take their luggage.

"Thanks for driving us so carefully," Tessa said.

"No problem. Give a ring when you want me to bring you back." Serge waved and drove off.

The porter accompanied them to the reception desk, where they were signed in and were allocated two rooms on the first floor just three doors away from each other.

"Let's go down to lunch after we've unpacked, then we can plan what we want to do. Meet in my room in an hour?" Tessa said as they parted.

"Fine," Ana said. "Could we make it a bit longer? I'm not as quick as you."

Tessa laughed. "Okay, make it an hour and a half."

Tessa explored her room. There was a standard sized double bed with just room for two easy chairs. To her surprise, on the bedside table there was a nine-inch computer tablet. She switched it on, and the screen lit up with the message, "Welcome to the Hotel Wiltshire. We have free Wi-Fi. To find out the attractions of Bern, feel free to surf the web."

Switching it off, she went through her usual routine of bouncing on the bed and checking the pillows. *Hmm, not quite up to the Splendide's standard, but not bad. Quite a small bathroom.* She had a quick wash, noting that the towels were fine but not as large and fluffy as the ones at the Splendide. She began unpacking. Bella, her doll, lay on the top of her clothes and was carefully placed sitting up on the bed while Tessa put the rest of her things away. After unpacking, she looked at the time. Still half an hour to go before Ana was due to come and see her, so to while away the time she switched on the computer tablet again and brought up a web page on what to do in Bern. She spent the time clicking on various attractions.

There was a knock on the door. It was Ana.

"Come in. Look what I found by my bed." Tessa held up the tablet.

"I found one too," Ana said. "I was quite surprised. I suppose it only works in the hotel, otherwise people would make off with them?"

Tessa turned it over. "Look there's a note on the back, *Please do not remove this tablet from your room. A similar model which works outside this hotel can be purchased from reception.* That explains it. Anyway, have you looked at it yet?"

Ana sat down in one of the chairs and sighed. "No, I'm no good with computers. What did you find out?"

"I've only just switched it on. Tell you what, let's look at it together after lunch. I'll switch off again for now." Tessa looked at her watch. "We'd better go down. Shall we just have a sandwich?" Ana agreed and they made their way down in the lift.

Tessa asked at reception and was told that a light lunch was served in the lounge.

Over lunch they discussed what they remembered from the last time they were here.

"I expect things have changed a bit. It was two years ago, wasn't it? I remember you falling for that waiter in the . . . What was the name of the restaurant?" Tessa smiled.

Ana blushed. "I don't remember, and I didn't fall for him. I wouldn't anyway, as Hans and I have been sweethearts since we were children."

Ana looked sad, and Tessa realised that her friend was thinking of Hans and had only agreed to come away with her out of friendship. What she really wanted was news of her sweetheart.

She put her hand on Ana's arm, "I'm sure he is all right," she said. "Serge will let us know if there's any news, and we'll be back in a day or two. Let's relax and enjoy ourselves. You need a break as much as I do."

Then she realised what she was doing. *I'm repeating a pattern. I'm running away from a man for the second time. What is it with me?*

She looked up to see Ana looking at her, a worried expression on her face.

"Are you all right?" she asked.

Tessa picked up her sandwich. "I was just thinking about something I haven't told you about. You remember my dip in the water? Well that wasn't the real reason I was so upset. I didn't want to tell you the whole story while Serge was there, but I can tell you now."

"I knew there was something more. Tell me."

"It's about Alex, the man I introduced you to the other

day."

Ana leant forward, her eyes opening wide. "He is your boyfriend?"

"Not really, but I have been seeing him. Then he invited me to lunch at his chateau. While we were walking in the garden a small boy ran up to him calling him *daddy*. I think he must be married. It was such a shock I just ran, and my first thought was to come to you, then Serge arrived so I couldn't tell you in front of him."

"You poor thing." Ana sympathised. "So that was why you wanted to get away from Zurich?"

"Yes, and it was good of you to suggest coming with me especially as you are so worried about Hans."

"Let's forget about men for a day or two and concentrate on enjoying ourselves."

Tessa knew that Ana was putting on a brave face. She finished her tea, stood up and said, "Fine, let's go back to my room."

As soon as they reached Tessa's room, Ana shut the door firmly and bounded on to the bed.

"Now it's time for me to comfort you," she said, flinging off her clothes." She sat naked and pulled Tessa towards her.

Tessa put her hands up in front of her laughing. "No, no," she said, conscious that the sight of Ana's petite body was doing things to her insides. She learnt forward, kissing Ana, and then unable to help herself, kissed Ana's tiny nipples. Ana squirmed and reached for the buttons on Tessa's blouse. Soon Tessa was as naked as Ana, and they lay together on the bed exchanging kisses.

"I love you," Ana said, caressing Tessa's breasts. "It's funny that we can love each other in this way, and yet I love my sweetheart very much. You must find yourself a man."

Tessa ran her hands down Ana's body. "I've had enough of men since I walked out on Rob, but it is true you can love both a man and a woman. One day, perhaps the right man may come along." She stopped talking and gave Ana a loving kiss.

Sometime later, their bodies still entwined, they kissed once more and then sat up.

"We must dress and plan the rest of our holiday." Tessa smoothed down her hair.

After dressing Tessa switched on the computer tablet and brought up *Things to do in Bern.*

They both pored over the screen. The first thing that came up was the invitation to swim in the river.

"The last thing I want to do is swim after my last experience." Tessa shuddered.

"How about a stroll through the town?" Ana asked. "Just to get the feel of the place again."

"Good idea, let's do that tomorrow. This afternoon I just want to be lazy. I've brought a book with me. We don't really need to look at this do we?" Tessa turned off the tablet and set it on the bedside table. "What do you think?"

"That's fine," Ana said. "We can talk about what to do for the rest of the days over dinner tonight. I noticed some magazines in the foyer. I'll read, too. I might even have a snooze. How about meeting for tea later?"

"That suits me fine. Say four o'clock? I'll call for you."

When Ana had gone, Tessa took out her book, moved her doll onto the side table and curled up on the bed to read. After a while the idea of a snooze seemed attractive and she fell asleep, the book dropping from her hand.

She woke with a start, to someone knocking gently on her door. It was Ana.

The door was not locked, so Ana came in, standing in the doorway laughing. "Wake up, it's gone four o'clock. I thought

I was the one going to have a snooze."

"It must be the mountain air," Tessa said, blinking.

"Come on, let's go down for tea."

Tea was a pleasant interlude, and the rest of the day went quickly. Ana had a phone call on her mobile from Serge saying that he had got back to Zurich. No news of Hans yet, but he would keep in touch.

When they went down for dinner, the dining room of the hotel reminded Tessa of the dining room of the Titanic as she remembered it from the film, all glass chandeliers, small tables, people talking excitedly. Waiters dressed in crisp, smart uniforms circulated among the guests.

They enjoyed their meal and were happy in each other's company. They took coffee in the lounge and then went off to their respective rooms.

Next morning Tessa woke up hearing a light tap on the door. Slipping on the flimsy housecoat provided by the hotel, Tessa staggered sleepily to unlock and open the door. It was Ana, up and fully dressed.

"Wake up, sleepyhead." Ana sat down, regarding Tessa who was trying to clear the sleep from her eyes.

"That's the best sleep I've had for a while." Tessa sat on the edge of the bed, yawning.

"That's what getting away from it all means." Ana got up. "I'll leave you to get dressed. Come along to my room when you're ready, and we'll go down for breakfast."

Tessa nodded as Ana let herself out, then left her doll on the side table, mindful that the maid would be making the bed.

She got ready and made her way to Ana's room.

In the dining room Tessa unusually decided to have a full breakfast and so tucked into sausage, bacon and egg, while Ana just had cheese and brown bread.

After breakfast Tessa said, "See you down in the lobby in ten minutes. Don't forget, it's cold out there, wrap up warm."

As they went out into the street, the concierge opened the glass doors for them, then standing outside, he stamped his feet trying to keep warm.

Clad in their warm coats, hats and scarves, they ventured into the cobbled streets of the old town. As they passed the concierge, he saluted. They went on, trying to keep warm in spite of the cold.

People hurried past them, intent on their tasks, hurrying to work, no-one dawdling, it was too cold. Everyone's breath came out like miniature fog.

"I remember this," Tessa said, as they walked through the medieval shopping arcades of the Kramgasse.

The old buildings, mellowed with age, caught the sunlight as it flooded down onto the street.

"It seems a bit warmer now we're walking under the covered arcades. You would think it would be better to walk out in the sun." Ana pulled her scarf closer.

Then, as they passed a patisserie, the smell of freshly baked bread wafted towards them.

Tessa drew a deep breath, "That smells good. It's a pity we can't take some bread back with us."

They passed on leisurely down the street.

Ana looked in a shop window displaying slabs of chocolate. "We must buy some chocolate while we're here. That, we can take back."

Time passed as they strolled, looking in windows of drugstores, bakeries, jewellery stores, and bookstores, until Tessa stopped. "I need to sit down. How about a coffee and one of the wonderful pastries they make?"

"If I remember, there's a place just a bit farther on." Ana pointed ahead. "There, on the left."

They walked into a book café where all sorts of gorgeous

looking pastries were displayed. A waitress took their order, allowing them to choose from the wide selection displayed.

"I'm having Meitschibei," Ana said, pointing at a horse-shoe shaped pastry. "It's good, you should try it. It's a croissant filled with sweetened hazelnuts."

Tessa looked doubtful but allowed herself to be persuaded. Their coffee and the croissants arrived.

"It's terrific," Tessa said, biting into it. "If I eat enough pastries I'm not going to want any lunch."

"Have we got time to look around the bookshop?" Ana asked, drinking the last of her coffee.

"All the time in the world. We're on holiday." Tessa sighed with satisfaction.

They spent some time looking round the shop. Tessa found a section of English books and was tempted to buy a romance that took her fancy when she was pulled away by Ana. "Come on. We're sightseeing, not buying things."

Tessa laughed. "I'll remind you of that when we get near the chocolate."

Arm in arm, they marched down the street.

"Since we're sightseeing I must take you to see the Zytglogge," Ana said.

"What's that?"

"It's Bern's famous clock tower. Come, I'll show you."

They turned off the main road and down a side alley which led to a pillared fountain surmounted by the figure of a helmeted warrior, a bear at his feet. Behind it was a magnificent clock tower.

"It's a clock tower now, but it used to be a gate tower for the city and then a prison." Ana pointed at the tower which sported two clocks, one an astrological face showing signs of the zodiac and the other a more conventional, larger clock face above it.

"We can go in to see the mechanism if you like, everybody

does." Ana turned to Tessa and then stepped back in surprise as a tall man came up behind Tessa and tapped her lightly on the shoulder.

Tessa swung round, tensing up, then relaxed. "Alex, what are you doing here?" Her heart gave a sudden leap.

"I've come to see you," he said. "I couldn't have you running off like that the other day without waiting for an explanation."

For a moment Tessa couldn't think what to say, then collecting her wits she said, "How did you know I was here?"

"Ah, well, you told reception at the Splendide where you were going. As they know me well they were happy to tell me. I tried your hotel here, but they said you had gone for a walk and since everyone ends up at the Zytglogge, I thought I would try here first, and I was right."

He moved them gently out of the stream of tourists queuing to go into the clock tower.

Alex turned to Ana, grasping her hand. "Hi, Ana. Good to see you again."

Ana smiled. "We were just going into the clock tower ourselves. Would you like to join us?"

Alex looked across at Tessa. "I rather hoped I could steal Tessa from you for a moment so that I could ask her forgiveness and explain what happened the other day, but I do have some news for you as well."

"I don't have any secrets from Ana, so say whatever you wanted to say, since you've come all this way," Tessa said abruptly, the memory of their last encounter still strong in her mind.

"That's fine, if you want it that way, but let me buy you both lunch and we can talk." Alex took her remarks in a calm and controlled way.

"I don't see that there's much to talk about." Tessa found herself getting worked up, her anger returning. She took no notice of the startled looks of the people crowding round to get into the clock tower.

Alex dragged her clear of the crowd. Ana followed them.

"Come on," he said. "Let's go to Einstein's Haus. It's just round the corner in the Kramgasse."

They went into the warm cave-like interior of the café and were shown to a table in the corner. The waitress came and took their order.

As she left, Tessa said, "I'm not sure I'm in a mood to listen to you. We came away for a relaxing holiday, and now you've followed us here and spoilt it."

"I had to." Alex clasped his hands together in an attitude of prayer. "I know what it looked like, a young boy calling me *daddy*, a young woman looking after him, but it wasn't what you imagined."

"Well, then what was it like?"

"Are you sure you want me to stay?" Ana looked concerned. "I can go for a walk if you like?"

Tessa touched Ana's arm. "No, stay, let's both hear his explanation."

Alex hesitated as though he didn't know how to begin, then it came out like a flood. "The boy is my eight-year-old son, his name is Luka. My wife died in childbirth."

"And so you married again?"

"Of course not, how could I and now I've met you . . ." Alex's words tailed off as he looked at Tessa as though to beg her forgiveness.

Ana looked from Alex to Tessa, nodding as though she understood.

Tessa still didn't look convinced. "And what about the attractive young woman I saw on the path?"

Alex squirmed a little. "That's Maria, I employ her as Luka's nanny."

The sandwiches and tea that they had ordered arrived.

Ana said, "Shall I pour?"

"Yes please." Tessa felt as though a river that had been dammed up was suddenly released. She turned away, tears welling up in her eyes. She knew that Alex had noticed, so she wiped her eyes and turned to him. "I don't know what to say," she said, "You came all this way to find me?"

"Yes, I had to, but more than that." Alex turned to Ana. "I have news of your Hans."

Ana clasped her hands together. "Is he all right?"

"As far as we know he was taken to our mountain research centre by my partner, Eric, but as I told you, all communication with them has been cut off."

"So how did you find out?" Ana looked appealingly at him.

"It was luck, really. My receptionist there, Sally, has a mobile phone. We don't often get a signal for mobiles on the mountain top, but as luck would have it she managed to phone me. Hans has been up there since he disappeared, and my partner Eric Weber is with him. I'll be having strong words with that man when I see him."

"I've been meaning to ask you—why on earth put a research station on top of a mountain?" Tessa was feeling light-headed after hearing everything he'd told them.

Alex turned to her. "I can't answer that now, but believe me there is a reason. Maybe I can tell you later." He reached out and held her hands across the table. "In any case I must go there to see what is going on. I flew here in the company helicopter. Would you like to come with me? "

"Well, we're booked into the Hotel Wiltshire for two more days. This is only the first day of our holiday. What do you think, Ana?"

Ana, who had been sitting back listening, leant forward. "I'd love a helicopter ride."

Tessa gave him a thoughtful look, her heart still jumping

for joy, then said, "Yes, but we must let the hotel know."

"We can do that, then I have to fly back to Zurich before we go on to the research centre, " Alex said. "I've got some things to sort out, but it won't take long, and we can take you up the mountain after that. Come and cancel your hotel. I'll help you collect your cases."

"Is that all right, Ana?" Tessa looked at her friend.

"This holiday is turning into an adventure, and if finding Hans is at the end of it I'm all in favour." Ana's eyes twinkled as she smiled.

CHAPTER SIX

"Right, that's decided," Alex said decisively as he beckoned the waitress and paid the bill. On the short walk back to the hotel, he explained that the helicopter was waiting at the airfield just outside Bern.

When they reached the hotel, Tessa was surprised to find that the manager made no objection to the cancellation and indeed seemed pleased that he had rooms free for more guests.

"As I told you, mademoiselle, we are full up and I have been turning people away, so thank you for letting me know. I will send porters up for your luggage when you are ready."

"I'll wait here until you come down." Alex settled himself into one of the comfortable chairs in the lounge as Tessa and Ana went up to their rooms.

They came down with the porters carrying their cases.

The manager, all smiles, saw them off as they piled into a waiting taxi and their cases were put in the back.

Alex gave the taxi driver instructions and they set off to the airfield. The taxi took them to the private part of the airfield where Stephan, Alex's chauffeur, was waiting by a powerful-looking helicopter.

"Hi, Stephan, are you the pilot?" Tessa greeted him. "Is there anything you can't drive?"

Stephan smiled. "I can manage most things except perhaps a bicycle. Come, I've dealt with the formalities, so we're ready to go."

Alex looked admiringly at him " He can also pilot the

firm's Lear jet. A very useful man to have around," Alex helped them in.

The helicopter was comfortably able to seat the three of them and the pilot. They settled in, Alex sitting by Stephan, Tessa and Ana in the back.

The helicopter took off smoothly, rising into the air like a giant bird. It circled once over the airfield and then set off in the direction of Zurich.

Ana was thrilled by the ride, looking down as the scene below unfolded. Tessa was looking at Alex rather than the scenery until suddenly there was a jolt and the sound of the engine died.

Alex, turned round to Tessa and Ana. "A slight emergency," he yelled. "Don't worry, Stephan can handle it."

The helicopter bucked alarmingly like a horse determined to throw its rider.

Stephan fought the controls as they lost height.

"Are we going to crash?" Ana clutched Tessa's arm.

As Stephan seemed to regain, control Alex turned to reassure them.

"Don't worry, it doesn't happen often, and Stephan is trained for this. It's going to be a bit bumpy, but he's using what we call autorotation. Even though we've lost the engine, the rotor blades will continue to spin, he'll get the pitch of the blades right and we'll come down like a parachute." He glanced over to Stephan, who waved reassuringly as they descended at what Tessa thought was an alarming rate, the whole vehicle spinning like a top in a whirlwind.

"I'm feeling sick." Ana clutched Tessa even tighter.

Tessa looked out of the window. "The ground seems to be coming up very fast," she said, as they crash-landed in someone's garden, jolting them almost out of their seats, although their seat belts held them.

Tessa looked out and could see that the crashing helicopter

had narrowly missed landing in a small swimming pool but instead had landed in a flower bed.

Tessa and Ana were both shaking as Alex helped them out.

The owner of the house quickly arrived, looking in horror at the wreckage of his garden, his flower bed destroyed beyond recognition.

As Stephan climbed out, Alex hurried across to the house owner. "My apologies, sir," he said. "We had engine failure ,but fortunately my pilot was able to land us safely, although it has caused a bit of damage to your garden. "

Anyone else would have objected to the term *a bit of damage* when it looked as if a large portion of the garden had been wrecked, but Tessa thought the man seemed very calm, almost too calm. She hugged Ana to comfort her as the man waved towards the house. "You had better come in out of the cold."

"I really am sorry about this," Alex said. "I'll make sure all this is put right as soon as we can move my machine."

"Don't worry about that now," the man said. "Come on in, you all look a bit shaken. My wife will look after the girls." Then, as his wife, a tall willowy blonde, appeared, he asked, "Alice, can you help, my love?"

With an expression of horror on her face, Alice looked at the wreckage of their garden and then, composing herself, said, "Of course, come on in, I'll get you a nice cup of tea."

Tessa and Ana, still shaken, followed her into the house.

Stephan went over to Alex. "I've shut everything down so it should be safe now. I'll need to take a look at what's wrong and see if I can fix it."

"I'm really sorry about this," Alex said, shaking the owner's hand. "These two ladies are Tessa and Ana. I was just giving them a lift back to Zurich when this happened. but thanks to our gallant pilot, Stephan, no bones were broken. I'm Alex Baxter."

"Harry Kendle," the man said. "You both look as if you could do with something stronger than tea, come on in. You say it's safe to leave your machine?"

"Yes, apart from the damage to your flower bed, it'll be fine," Stephan reassured him.

"It's not every day one has a helicopter growing in the garden," Harry said, as he poured them liberal measures of whisky.

As soon as he had downed his whisky, Stephan excused himself and went back out to the helicopter. He soon came back, shaking his head. "I'm sorry, but the problem is more major than I thought. There's no way we can move it at the moment."

"Don't worry about it, have some more whisky."

Stephan refused politely and turned to Alex. "If you like, I'll get on the phone to get some transport to get us to Zurich. We may have to leave the machine here for a while."

"I'll show you where the phone is." Harry took Stephan out as Alice came in with tea and biscuits.

Tessa looked round as she was handed her tea. It was a homely room, with worn armchairs and a piano in the corner with a number of photographs standing on it. One in particular caught Tessa's attention, a framed photo of a man standing by what looked like a Spitfire.

As Harry came back into the room he saw her looking. "Yes, that was me. No, I wasn't in World War Two, I'm not that old, but a few of us got together, rescued the old crate, repaired it, and flew it a bit at air shows."

"So, you're a pilot?" Alex said. "I wondered why you took a helicopter landing in your garden so calmly."

Harry laughed, looking at his wife. "Retired now, of course, but I used to fly Hercules in the RAF. Came here for the mountain air, but our son's a pilot." He pointed proudly to another photograph on the sideboard.

Stephan came back saying that he had ordered a taxi for them.

After a short interval the taxi came. Stephan rescued Tessa and Ana's cases from the helicopter, loading them into the taxi. They all said their goodbyes and thanks, Alex promising to get the helicopter removed and make good any damage to the garden.

It was mid-afternoon when Alex dropped Tessa and Ana at Ana's apartment.

"Change of plan now, I think. The helicopter is going to be out of service for quite a while."

Stephan nodded his agreement.

"I'll keep in touch and let you know what's happening."

"I thought we were going to find Hans." Ana sounded disappointed as they walked into her apartment. Alex and Stephan had gone on to their headquarters.

Tessa tried to console her. "If Hans is up there on the mountain, at least he's safe, and Alex will do his best to get us there. Don't worry."

The afternoon stretched into evening but there was no call from Alex.

"Something must have happened." Ana could see that Tessa was looking worried. "Alex has your mobile number, doesn't he?"

"Yes, he does, do you think I should phone him?"

"Better not, he may be in the middle of something. I'm sure he'll get in touch when he's free. I think I'll give Serge a ring just to keep him in the picture."

Ana rang Serge, who was surprised that they were back in Zurich already, but pleased that Hans had been traced.

"I'm making a meal," Ana said. "Why don't you come over and share it with us?"

"That's great, I'd like to," Serge said. "Is Tessa with you?"

"Yes, she is. Perhaps you could take her back to her hotel afterwards. It doesn't look as though we shall be going anywhere tonight."

Serge arrived as Ana was preparing a simple meal for the three of them.

While they were eating, Alex rang Tessa's mobile apologising for not getting back to them before.

"It's one thing after another," he said. "We've just lost a shipment of plastic, so I've had to spend time chasing that, and now I've just heard that our helicopter is out of service for at least two weeks. I was hoping to go to our research centre tomorrow, but I'll have to arrange something else. Stephan won't be able to drive us as he's tied up with his helicopter arrangements."

When Tessa told them what Alex had said, Serge immediately volunteered. "Why don't I drive you?"

"Oh, Serge, you can't go driving us around all the time," Ana said.

"I enjoy driving, let me do it," he said.

"Go on, Ana, let him drive us. I'll tell Alex, he'll enjoy Serge's driving."

Serge looked at her. "Was that a joke?" he asked.

Tessa smiled. "Let me phone Alex."

"That might work very well, "Alex said when she phoned, "What's Serge's driving like?"

"I think you'll find it all right." She smiled at Serge.

"Right, can we make it tomorrow as planned?"

"Is tomorrow all right, Serge, about ten o'clock setting off from the hotel?"

"Fine, I'll pick you up, then go round to Ana's. Will Alex come to the hotel?"

"I think he will, I'll ask him." Tessa said.

Next day Serge picked Tessa and Alex up at the hotel.

As they drove to collect Ana, Serge said, "The road to Grindelwald may be a bit treacherous, it has been snowing quite a bit."

Alex looked at him sharply.

"Don't worry. I'm used to driving in snowy conditions and I have got a satnav," Serge said.

Alex heaved a sigh. "Okay, but remember you're carrying a precious cargo." He looked across at Tessa.

Alex was sitting in the front with Serge. Ana slipped in the back with Tessa.

Serge's car smelt of old leather, and the blue seat coverings were showing signs of wear. Serge swung into the main stream of traffic. "Everyone all right there?" he asked, craning his neck round.

"We're fine," Tessa said. "We've fastened our seat belts."

"Hang on then." Serge put his foot down on the accelerator and the car surged forward.

Serge seemed to have a psychic understanding of the road and its conditions as he drove full speed towards Grindelwald.

As they got near to the village, the road turned icy. Snow was falling in gentle flakes blown sideways by the wind. The windscreen wipers were just about coping.

Tessa was glad when they reached their destination, as Serge's driving and his control of the vehicle were excellent, but the speed with which he drove was enough to worry even a racing driver.

Tessa got out stiffly, stretching her legs, then went round to help Ana out.

Alex stayed in the car for a moment having a word with Serge.

When he got out, he said, "Serge's going to wait for us in the cafe, then he'll drive us back to Zurich when we come down. Now we are taking a train trip, come on." He led them over to the cogwheel train station.

"That's odd," he said as he purchased tickets. "We go on this train, but we have to get up by lift for the final stage which takes us to the research centre and the observatory at the very top. I've just been told that the lift service has been suspended and there's no other way to get to the top."

"So that means we can't go?" Ana asked.

"Yes, we can. Once we've reached the end of the train ride I'm sure I can find some way to get us to the top," Alex said confidently.

"How long does the train take?" Tessa asked, looking at him admiringly.

"Just over an hour," Alex replied. "But you'll enjoy the ride."

Ana looked uncertain. "Why so long? I don't like heights," she said. "How high is it?"

Alex replied, "Over three thousand metres. It takes a long time as it is quite slow and the train winds around both inside and outside the mountain."

Ana shuddered and drew her heavy coat around her.

"You don't have to look out. The only thing is you might feel a bit queasy on the last stretch. That's quite normal if you go over two thousand metres." He smiled at Tessa as though to say *we must look after her.*

"I'm not sure I like this," Ana murmured.

Tessa put her arm around her. "You'll be all right, we're with you."

The cogwheel train was standing in the station. Snow was falling fast now. People were boarding the four-carriage train, its green and yellow livery standing out stark against the snowy background. They found seats in the first compartment.

"I like sitting near the front," Alex said. "You get a better view." He patted the seat next to him for Tessa to sit close. "I hope you're going to be warm enough," he said, pulling her coat closer for her.

At his touch Tessa felt a thrill run through her body.

Ana huddled down in her seat looking miserable, but once the train set off she straightened up, looking out of the window, exclaiming in delight at the view.

Tessa was also impressed as the lower slopes with pine trees laden with snow passed slowly before their eyes. Higher and higher the train climbed slowly, wending its way round until it turned inside the mountain, stopping at a vantage point where passengers could take photographs of the magnificent view of snowy peaks and mountains outside.

"I'd forgotten about the stop," Alex said impatiently.

Tessa jumped up. "I'd like to get out and have a look."

"All right, I'll come with you." Alex sounded reluctant but he got up. "Glancing back he asked, "Will you be all right, Ana?"

Ana huddled further into her coat. "Yes, I'm fine, you two go."

The vantage point was a large, jagged hole in the rock. Most people had got out of the train to look out at the mountains beyond.

"There's actually not much to see at the moment." Alex craned to over people's heads. "Looks like a heavy mist. Here let me get you to the front."

He carefully manoeuvred Tessa through to the front, apologising to other people as he did so.

The mist cleared for a second as Tessa looked out, and the view across the valley with the snow-clad peaks behind was magnificent. She felt a sensation almost like flying. As she turned to Alex the mist came down again and everything was blanked out.

"Come on, let's get back to the train." Alex pulled her out of the mass of spectators.

They settled back in their seats and the train whistle sounded, a strange spooky sound, echoing back from the rocky walls as people rushed back aboard.

On reaching the top, everyone climbed out onto the rocky platform, Tessa could see that some people weren't properly dressed for the weather and were feeling the cold. Others were clad in sensible arctic gear.

Alex helped the two of them down onto the platform, but Tessa noticed that he held onto her hand a little longer than he did with Ana.

"Come on," he said. "Let's see if that lift is in operation."

They made their way through a rocky tunnel decorated with stars which made it seem less stark than it would otherwise have been. Most people were heading for the exhibition and café areas, but some went towards the large glass doors of the lift. A notice hung at the side regretting that the lift was out of order. There were groans of disappointment.

Alex paused in front of the notice. "I don't believe this."

He looked towards the café area. "Wait for me, I won't be long."

He pushed his way through the crowd of disappointed tourists and was soon back, dragging with him a small man in a uniform who took the notice from the lift door, turned a key in the control panel and stepped inside.

"Stand back ladies and gentlemen." The man held up his hand as the small crowd surged forward. "I have to test to see if the lift is working properly. We shouldn't be long."

He ushered Tessa, Ana and Alex quickly into the lift and closed the doors against the crowd. The lift began to rise.

As they stepped out at the higher level, Alex passed something to the lift man, patting him on the back. The man stepped back inside, and the lift descended.

"What did you do? The little man seemed frightened to death," Tessa asked as they walked along the rocky passage towards a set of glass doors with the words Roboplastix Inc engraved on them.

"He'd been bribed by Weber to suspend the lift service." Alex said. "I had a quiet word with him."

"Not so quiet." Tessa laughed. "What about all the people stranded up here?"

"I asked him about that. He told me he had made sure that all the tourists were down on the other level before stopping the service."

"But your research people are still up here," Ana broke in.

Alex smiled. "True, but you see they were still working, and our research centre is fully equipped for all emergencies. We can hold out here for ages and if necessary could escape by skiing down the mountain."

Tessa looked puzzled. "Why on earth have a research centre at the top of an almost inaccessible mountain?"

Alex put his arm around her and gave her a little squeeze. "Perhaps it's time to let you into the secret, come and see. I think it will surprise you."

The research centre was a low, purpose-built building nestling on a wide ledge, accessed by the passage inside the mountain that they had walked down.

He led the way inside, through the glass doors, pausing at the reception desk.

The receptionist looked up. "Mr Baxter. We certainly weren't expecting to see you. We've been cut off for a while. How did you get here, with the lift out of action?"

Tessa glanced at Alex who smiled and said, "Just a little misunderstanding, Sally. It must have been quite frightening for you all, but I had a word with the lift operator, and everything is back to normal now."

The receptionist gave a sigh of relief. "I'll tell the others," she said, reaching for her intercom.

Alex leant on the desk. "Is Mr Weber in?"

She nodded. "Shall I page him for you?"

"No, I'll get to him later. I'd like to show our little establishment to our visitors first. Are there any other visitors here with you?"

The receptionist turned to her computer screen, punching some keys. "Yes, a Mr Richter. He's been up here for a few days. He's around somewhere."

As she spoke Ana gave a little cry and darted forward. A smallish man dressed in a sports jacket and slacks came out of a side passage. As he saw Ana, a smile spread across his face, and he rushed towards her.

"Hans," Ana cried, throwing herself into his arms, her eyes sparkling.

"Ana, my darling," he said, hugging her tightly. "I'm sorry if you were worried about me. We had no means of letting you know I was all right until Sally here," he indicated the receptionist, "managed to phone out on her mobile phone and even then we didn't know if the signal got through."

Sally looked up. "We were lucky, as most of the time it doesn't work up here. Also, I don't know why the ordinary phones stopped working. Probably a fault on the line somewhere down the mountain."

"Don't we have a radio transmitter?" Alex asked.

"We did until someone smashed it," she said.

"So you were completely cut off?" Alex frowned. "Thanks Sally, come on the rest of you, let's get something to eat. I'm sure we can all do with some food and a cup of tea."

"I've just eaten," Hans said. "But I'll come with you." He didn't seem to want to let Ana go.

Alex led the way. "Remember," he said. "At this altitude, the tea won't be red hot."

"But it will be very welcome." Tessa loosened her coat, beginning to feel more relaxed in the warmer atmosphere.

They went into what seemed like a normal café. Some staff

were sitting at tables, obviously enjoying a break from their duties. Alex led Tessa to a table in the corner behind a massive artificial palm tree. Ana and Hans joined them.

As they sat down, he said, "We should be able to talk here. Let me get some tea first, but what would you like to eat?"

Ana said, "Just tea for me thanks." She seemed happy nestling in Hans's arms.

Tessa got up. "Let me come with you to see what they have."

Alex guided her to the counter. His nearness sent shivers down her spine. "You're cold," he said, putting his arm around her.

Tessa snuggled into his warm embrace, "No. I'm fine, but I think I'd like a donut." She pointed.

"I'll have the same," he said, ordering tea for the four of them and taking it back to the table.

Now that they were all settled and sustained by the warm liquid, Alex turned to Tessa. "You asked me why we put our centre on top of a mountain. I can't give you any details, but I can tell you we're doing research up here on a government contract, very hush hush."

Tessa looked round. "So that's why you put it up here. It's a pretty scary location."

"Yes it is, but it's convenient for the work we're doing. I was surprised that Weber brought Hans up here. I suppose he thought if he isolated him from the outside world, Hans would give up the secret of the new plastic."

He looked quizzically at Hans. "Why did you come up here, and did you give him the secret? From what I've seen, it's a pretty amazing substance."

Hans leant forward, his arm still around Ana's shoulders. "It is amazing, but no, I didn't tell him anything, although he has been pretty persistent. It was after I had completed the job for Roboplastix that Weber lured me up here with the promise of more work, then he went off leaving me here unable to get away. He came back yesterday to show me one of the dolls I had given Ana. I asked him how he had got it, but he refused to tell me. He just said he would be able to analyse a sample of the plastic now that he had the doll, so he didn't need me anymore. The way he said it was rather threatening, but yesterday he became friendly again as he said he had been unable to analyse the formula and still needed me to give it to him."

Ana hugged him. "I was so worried. Why couldn't you let me know what was happening?"

"Weber made sure we had no communication with the outside world. Even the staff couldn't leave. I told him it was useless keeping me here, as I don't know the secret of the plastic, but he didn't believe me."

They were all so engrossed in what Hans was saying that they failed to notice a figure coming up to them. It was Weber, a large, rough-looking man dressed in a stained lab coat, as he towered over them.

Ana pressed further into Hans's arms. "That's him," she whispered.

"Eric," Alex greeted him. "Where have you been?"

Weber's voice, when he spoke, was deep, harsh and impatient. "Never mind that now. I want you all to come with me urgently, I've got something to show you."

As he spoke Tessa looked at Alex who nodded. They left the table and followed Weber down the corridor to a door on the left.

"It's in here," he said, holding the door open for them. They went into the room which Tessa could see was furnished as a bedroom. Weber followed them in, locking the door.

As Tessa turned she saw what she first thought were two men standing to attention on either side of the door. They were standing without moving, almost as though they were statues.

"Meet my robot friends," Weber said, waving at them.

The robots moved to the doorway, blocking it. Their movements were smooth and easy, almost human like and yet in some way menacing.

"Weber. What are they doing in this section?" Alex asked in surprise. He turned to the others. "These are peacekeeping robots from the secret military project I told you about."

"I decided you weren't putting enough effort into the firm," Weber said. "So, I'm taking over, and when I get the secret of this plastic, these robots will be so lifelike no-one will know the difference between them and real humans. Now that you've brought little Ana here, I'm sure Hans is going to be cooperative." He lit a cigarette, waving the glowing tip in the air, and looked hard at Ana, who clutched Hans even tighter.

"You're crazy, we're leaving," Alex said, moving towards the door.

"No you're not, I'm keeping you all here until Hans tells me what he knows."

Hans stepped forward, Ana clinging to him. "Don't hurt Ana," he said. "I've told you before that I don't know the secret, but if you must know, it was invented by a friend of mine, Dr Anton Faure in his department at the University of Zurich. He wanted to try it out, so he gave me some to use on the dolls I was making for Ana."

"That's all I need to know," Weber smiled triumphantly. "I'm afraid you will all have to stay here while I talk to Dr Faure. I'll leave the two robots to keep you company."

He turned to the menacing figures. "You will keep these people here until I tell you to release them."

In unison the two robots replied, "We obey."

"Move away from the door, then guard them."

Weber unlocked the door and hurried out. The two robots moved back in front of the door, blocking the exit.

Tessa sat on the bed, looking at Alex. "Now what do we do?"

"Wait, and I'll show you." Alex joined Tessa on the bed and motioned Hans and Ana to sit in the two easy chairs on the far side of the room.

The two robots remained motionless.

Alex explained. "These robots are part of the military research project I told you about. Tessa and Ana, you've seen our domestic robots. These are a logical extension of our work. We're designing peacekeeping robots for use in various conflicts across the world. These two are prototypes and until now have been kept isolated in our special research wing."

"Does that mean we're stuck here until Weber releases us?" Tessa asked.

Ana looked frightened. "Is there nothing we can do? Hans you know this place, can we get out?"

"Not unless we can get through that door, and I don't think those robots are going to move."

Alex got up and went towards the robots. One of them lifted an arm threateningly.

He said, "You will obey me. Move to the end of the room and do not stop us from leaving this room."

The robot lowered its arm, and both of them moved away from the door.

"Quickly everyone, outside." Alex took Tessa's arm and pushed her into the corridor, closely followed by Hans and Ana. He closed the door and locked it.

"That won't hold them if they really want to get out," he said, "but it should give us a bit of time."

Tessa gasped. "How did you do that? I thought we were stuck there forever."

"Fortunately Eric forgot that the robots were programmed to respond to both our voices. I have as much control over these prototypes as he does." Alex walked them quickly down the corridor towards the reception area.

Sally was sitting at her desk, staring at the entrance doors which were still vibrating.

"Eric has just run out holding a doll," she said, catching her breath.

Alex ran out to the lift, but was too late, it had already started to go down. He turned back as the others came to meet him.

"I think your Dr Faure is in for a visit," Alex said.

"What can we do?" Tessa asked.

"Do you still have your mobile, Sally?" he asked.

She fished under the desk. "Yes, here it is, but I doubt if you'll get a signal."

Alex switched it on, but it was dead. "Well, as we can't phone out from here, we'll just have to get down to the village and warn the good doctor by phone from there. I'll get the lift back."

He went to the lift, pressing the button several times. "It's no good. Looks as if Weber has sabotaged the lift again. I'll try in a few minutes, but I don't think it will work."

"Well, that's it," Hans said. "Unless you can ski down?"

"That's the answer," Alex said. "Weber will be taking the cogwheel train, so if I ski down to the village and Serge drives me to Zurich, I can be at the University before Weber, catching him red handed."

"I'll come with you," Tessa said.

Alex looked at her in surprise. "You can ski?"

Tessa glanced at Ana. "Of course, Ana and I have skied all over the Alps."

"But not from this height, I'll bet." Alex shook his head.

"Well, no," Tessa admitted, "but I'm willing to try."

"I don't think I can risk you slowing me down. I must go." He turned.

Tessa caught his shoulder. "Better two of us. Come on."

Reluctantly, Alex said, "Right, come on, let's get to the equipment room."

He led the way to a room with skis and poles on a long rack, another rack with ski jackets, pants, and on the other side, a table laid out with helmets, goggles and gloves.

Alex shrugged into a ski jacket, but Tessa hesitated on choosing the colour of her jacket.

"Come on Tessa, we haven't got all day." Alex picked one off the rack. "Here, the blue one suits your colouring."

Tessa put it on, pulling a pair of ski pants over her slacks. Alex helped her to find ski boots and select suitable skis.

He handed her a small backpack. "Put anything you need when we reach the bottom in this, especially your shoes. You'll need them down there as it's impossible to walk in ski boots." He put his own shoes in a backpack.

Tessa took her shoes off and put them into the pack together with her shoulder bag.

Suitably kitted out with helmet, goggles, gloves and boots they made their way to the back of the building where there was a double door leading to a manmade platform.

Alex brushed the snow away from the door. "I hope you realise," he said, as they put their skis on, "this won't be like skiing down the piste, this is powder snow."

Tessa shivered slightly. "I know, I know, but I'll be all right."

Alex leant forwards and kissed her on the cheek. "Good luck."

"That was a cold kiss, can I have a warm one soon?" she said, stomping around in her boots to get the feel of them, before slotting her feet into the bindings of the skis. A final click, as she pressed down with her heels and the skis were on.

"I'll try to do better next time," Alex said, giving her a hug as she waved her ski poles and was off. Alex followed slightly behind, letting her get clear.

As he caught up with her it was obvious to Tessa that they were both experienced skiers, and although it would be quite a ride, it was possible.

CHAPTER SEVEN

The snow was deep. As they skied down, clouds of powdered snow followed their progress. Tessa took a little while to get used to skiing again but soon she was enjoying it and had an intense feeling of companionship as Alex skied beside her.

At first the going was easy. Then lower down they hit a bank of cloud when the world disappeared for what seemed a lifetime to Tessa. It was like travelling through wet cotton wool. She tensed up and had difficulty keeping her balance until she remembered something her ski instructor had taught her, *fool your body into feeling confident, sing a song, it will work.*

She felt her body relax as she hummed *Moon River,* and as she did so they emerged into brilliant sunlight.

The sun glistened on the snow, the clear blue sky contrasting with the snow-covered peaks around.

Gliding down this mountain must be one of the most incredible feelings a person can experience, almost like flying, she thought.

She gasped as Alex shot past her, the virgin snow hissing under the impact of his skis. He pointed with his ski pole to the left where she could see a line of pine trees.

"Follow me," he shouted.

Obediently she followed as he turned into the trees, zigzagging down.

She followed his lead through the pines. Suddenly she heard a crack and Alex fell.

She rushed down to him where he sat nursing his ankle. His ski had come off and had slid a short distance away.

"Are you all right?" Tessa gasped.

"Not really." He smiled ruefully. "I'm stupid, I hit a tree root. I think my ankle is gone."

Tessa shook off her skis, sinking into the snow as she put her arms round him, dragging him to sit upright against the tree that had floored him.

He looked up at her. "It's nice to be in your arms. We must do this more often."

"Don't joke. What are we going to do?"

"We're nearly down. The village isn't far." Alex said, grimacing in pain. "You go on. Get Serge. Go to the university as we planned. Send someone up to rescue me."

His shoulders sagged as Tessa went after his ski. She brought it back, hesitating. "Are you sure you can't walk? We could get you down to the village if it isn't far."

"No, I don't think I can stand." He tried to raise himself gingerly, putting his weight on his foot but collapsed in pain. "Look, it isn't snowing now so if you can get someone up here quickly, I shall be all right. You go on. It's important to get to Dr Faure and warn him."

Tessa buckled on her skis, stamping on the snow and setting off. She didn't dare turn and wave in case she lost her balance. *I mustn't fall, I mustn't fall, Alex is depending on me.*

The village came into sight. Making a sweeping turn to the left, she shrugged off her skis, shook the snow from her boots, took them off, opened her backpack, and taking out her shoes walked into the main street.

She knew that Serge would be in the café, so she went there first. He was sitting at a table by the window, toying with a coffee.

He stood up rapidly as she approached, spilling his coffee. "Hi, where's Alex and the others?"

"It's a long story," she said. "Alex is stuck up the mountain by some trees. I think his ankle is broken. We must get help to him, and then we have to get back to Zurich quickly. I'll explain more after we've got help for Alex."

Serge acted quickly. "I noticed a mountain rescue office just down the street. Come on, leave your skis here, they won't mind." He called the waitress over.

She took the skis and Tessa's backpack. "Don't worry," she said. "I'll keep them safe for you."

At the mountain rescue office, a friendly officer questioned Tessa closely, taking notes, as she explained what had happened. Two men were immediately given instructions, taking a stretcher and other equipment, leaving in the direction that she had indicated and following the tracks she had made.

"We have to go back to Zurich," Tessa told the officer. Suddenly she swayed slightly as the strain of the journey down and the urgency of the situation caught up with her. "Will he be all right if we leave him with you?"

"Of course," the officer said. "We'll look after him, but you look all in yourself. Would you like to rest before you move on? We're very used to these situations."

"No, I'm fine, we must go. Come on, Serge."

"Well, if you're sure." The officer looked dubious but saw that Tessa was determined.

"The car's parked down the road." Serge helped Tessa out of the office.

After piling into Serge's old car, they set off at speed. At first Tessa didn't register much about the journey as she was still feeling disorientated.

Serge drove in his usual fashion, using his satnav to find his way through the streets of Zurich to get to the university.

As Tessa gradually recovered, she told Serge the story of what had happened.

"I'm a bit afraid he might get there before us," she said with a worried expression on her face.

"We're all right for time. If he's had to come down on that train, as you said, there's no way he can beat us to it." Serge sought to reassure her." We'll get to Dr Faure well ahead of Weber, don't worry."

They arrived at the University, and Serge parked the car in what looked like a reserved space in front of the main building. Leaping out before anyone could tell them to move it, they went in the main entrance.

The reception desk was manned by two porters. Tessa explained that they wanted to see Dr Faure, thinking that they would ask questions about their business, but the sight of a pretty girl seemed enough to convince them, and fortunately Dr Faure was in his office and not in a lecture.

One porter showed them the way while the other phoned through to let him know they were coming.

Dr Faure's room was small, packed with books, papers all over the desk and some on the floor. The figure behind the desk rose as they entered. Dr Faure was a giant of a man with long hair and whiskers. Cigarette ash spread over his egg-spotted waistcoat.

Tessa quickly introduced herself and Serge, explaining that they were friends of Hans and Ana.

"Sit down, sit down," Faure boomed. "Glad to meet friends of my friend. What can I do for you?"

Tessa looked round. The only two chairs in the room were covered in books.

"Push them off." Faure waved his hand. "Put them on the floor. A few more added to those already there won't make much difference." His eyes twinkled.

"We understand that you have perfected a new flexible plastic," Tessa began nervously.

Faure narrowed his eyes. "And where did you hear about

that? It's not generally known. I haven't patented it yet."

"You gave some to Hans, to use for his dolls." Serge still stood, unwilling to throw books onto the floor.

"Sit down, boy, sit down. Books won't bite you. Of course, I remember now, but what's the problem? He wasn't going to sell them, they were for his sweetheart, Ana. I wanted to test the plastic to make sure it didn't degrade so it seemed an ideal opportunity. "

Tessa leant forward,. "One of the dolls was stolen by a man called Eric Weber. We believe he tried to analyse the plastic, but he seems to have failed, so now he's on his way here to try to steal the formula from you."

"Well he can't have it, and he won't succeed." Faure chuckled. The phone rang. "Excuse me a moment." He spoke into the phone. "Yes, that's correct." He replaced the receiver. "Sorry about that."

"This is serious. He's on his way now," Tessa said, rocking back and forth on her chair.

"So what do you suggest, young lady?"

"It depends what he does." Tessa paused in thought.

Faure came out from behind his desk. "I think you'd better see my lab. You will find I am completely protected." He lumbered over to the glass panelled door and opened it. "Come, it's only next door."

Tessa and Serge followed him into a spacious room with lab benches spread with many different kinds of glass apparatus and electrical black boxes.

Tessa looked round. "I'm very much at home in these surroundings," she said, fingering a flask containing a pale pink liquid.

"How so?" Faure asked.

"I'm a research lecturer in chemistry at the University of Brookshire in England."

Faure settled his bulk on one of the benches, looking at her closely. "Hmm, they're getting younger and younger. Good for you, I know your Head of Department, Tom Neally."

Tessa smiled. "He's a good boss, but what about your plastic?"

Faure waved his hand round the room. "This is where it was developed, but I think I can reassure you. We have had trouble from intruders, before and most of the labs, this one included, are covered by video cameras that warn the security office if anyone comes in who is not entitled."

"How do they know if it's an intruder?" Serge asked.

"Facial recognition," Faure said. "Everyone who works here has their face registered."

"But we aren't registered?" Serge said.

"Your faces were photographed as you came in. That phone call was just checking that you were my guests."

"Fantastic." Serge looked up to the domed cameras in the corners of the room.

"It means that when your Mr Weber arrives, we can record it and you will be able to see in detail what happens." Faure picked up the phone. "I'll let security know what we want. In the meantime, you must be exhausted. " He looked at Tessa with concern.

Tessa had sagged against one of the benches, realising that she was still feeling the effects of the journey down the mountain and then Serge's fast drive back to Zurich.

"We have a good student cafeteria. You might like to wait there. I'll get someone to show you the way." Faure called to one of his students. "Frederick will show you the way, and afterwards, assuming this man comes, someone will call you and you can see what happened on the video replay."

Frederick, a fresh-faced boy still wearing his lab coat, led them to the cafeteria and then left them to go back to the lab.

Tessa sat down heavily on a chair while Serge went to the counter, ordering cake and coffee for them both.

"Do you think he really will come?" Serge put the tray down on the table, passing Tessa a piece of fruit cake and a coffee.

"Oh yes, he'll come. You didn't see the way he shot off after hearing Hans give the game away." Tessa nibbled her cake. "I only hope we don't have to wait too long. I'm worried about Alex."

"What about Ana and Hans?" Serge asked, picking up his coffee and putting it down again rapidly. "Ugh, they make their coffee hot."

Tessa smiled. "They'll be safe in Alex's research centre, and as soon as someone mends the lift they can come down."

Time passed and Tessa got fidgety, suggesting that they should go to Security to see what was happening.

They asked directions from the girl behind the counter and were directed to an office on the ground floor.

They knocked on a glass door marked *Security, No Entry*. There were two security men behind desks in the room. One got up, opened the door and let them in.

Serge explained who they were and one of the men said, "Your suspect is in with Dr Faure now. If you'd like to go in there," he indicated the room behind their desk, "we can show you a live picture on the screen."

Tessa thanked them. The room had a large viewing screen on the facing wall with chairs set in front of it. The display showed Weber in the laboratory with Dr Faure. Weber was holding up the doll he had brought with him, obviously questioning Faure about it. Tessa noticed that it's arm was damaged, presumably where Weber had taken a sample for analysis.

As they watched, they could see Weber becoming impatient. He threw the doll he'd been holding on to the floor.

Dr Faure stooped down and picked it up carefully, then set it down on one of the benches.

"It looks as if Weber is going to get violent, I think we ought to get up there in case anything happens." Serge went to the door and asked one of the security men the way back to Dr Faure's room. The men were watching their screen intently but didn't offer to go with them.

They hurried to the doctor's office. Watching events through the glass panelled door that led to the laboratory, they saw Weber grab a fire axe from the wall and bring it crashing down on some of the glass apparatus. Dr Faure cowered away from him.

Tessa and Serge looked on in horror as Weber threatened Faure with the axe.

There was a pause. Serge stepped forward as though to go in. Tessa held him back. "Wait," she breathed.

They saw Faure go to a wall cupboard and take out a sheaf of papers which he offered to Weber, who immediately grabbed them, hardly looking at them.

Serge looked across at Tessa. "I'm going in. Stay here."

He opened the door quietly. Weber had his back to him but at the last minute sensed that there was someone behind him. He turned. Serge grabbed him, holding onto the arm with the axe. Weber dropped the papers, twisting swiftly so that Serge was thrown back against the bench. As Weber raised the axe to strike, Tessa hurtled into the room, butting him in the back and throwing him off balance. Serge ducked desperately to the left as the axe crashed down and lodged in the bench.

The axe was hampering Weber and as he tried to regain his balance, the two security men burst into the room. He threw the axe at them. As they came towards him he ducked and ran from the room.

"He's getting away." Serge turned to run after him as several male students crowded into the room, alerted by the struggle.

Dr Faure, who had been standing quietly, his back against

a cupboard, put his hand on Serge's shoulder. "Let him go, I'll explain in a minute. It's all right you men, no problem, go back to work."

The students filed out, looking disappointed that there was no action. One of the security men picked up the axe while the other picked up the doll from the bench.

"What shall we do with this, doctor?" he asked, holding it out.

"I'll take it," Faure said, putting it back down on the bench.

He thanked the men and they left, after he agreed to fill in a report form for them.

He picked up the doll as he led Tessa and Serge back to his office. Wiping his brow, he motioned them to sit down. "That was quite a shock," he said. "Thank goodness for video cameras. You see, we are well protected."

Then he said to Serge, "You took a risk, young man, but thank you, I thank both of you."

"Why did you let him get away?" Serge asked. "He's got your formula."

Faure sat back smiling at them. "No, he only thinks he has. What I gave him was the report of a very early attempt at making it, which didn't work. If he tries to make it from that, he will be very disappointed, and if he sells it to someone else he will be in real trouble."

Serge shifted in his chair. "That may be so, but I think you ought to get your plastic patented as soon as possible and the police ought to be informed about this."

"Don't worry, Security will take care of that," Faure said, getting up and handing Tessa the doll. "You had better get this back to its rightful owner. I see it's been slightly damaged. When you see Hans, tell him I can repair it easily for him. I was pleased to see that, apart from that damage, there is no sign of degradation of the material. Now can I get you anything? Coffee, tea, or"—he looked at Serge—"something stronger?"

Serge got to his feet. "Thank you, but I think we must be going. Yes, Tessa?"

Tessa nodded her agreement. "Yes, I'm anxious about Alex, a friend of ours. We left him in a snow drift."

They shook hands with Dr Faure and left.

"I'm worried about this Weber character,' Tessa said as they walked out of the main entrance, "While he's still at large, there's no knowing what he will do."

"What can he do?" Serge walked towards the car.

"Well, when he finds out he's been tricked, he's bound to have another go to get the formula."

"Not from Dr Faure he won't. He's too well guarded."

"That means that Ana might still be in danger, as she will have the dolls."

"I don't think he'll try that again. Weber has already tried to analyse a sample and failed."

"I hope you're right." Tessa got into the car. "Are we going back now for Alex?"

"Yes, they should have rescued him by now." Serge swung the car back onto the road to Grindelwald.

As soon as they arrived, they went straight to the mountain rescue office.

The officer they had seen before greeted them and pointed to an inner room. "He's in there with the nurse."

The nurse turned as they entered.

"How is he?" Tessa asked.

Alex looked up at them from the bed he was lying on. He gave a weak grin.

"He'll be fine," she said. "Nothing is broken, just a bad sprain, but I've bound it up. You can take him home if you like."

"I'm fine," Alex said, trying to rise.

"Don't put too much weight on that foot," the nurse warned.

The nurse smiled at them both, and together with Tessa's help, eased Alex off the bed, and walked him gingerly into the main office.

When they came in, Serge said, "All set now. They will take care of the skis, including the ones you left in the café, and get them to the research centre when things are back to normal."

They said goodbye, thanking everyone. The nurse stood back as Tessa and Serge helped Alex into the car. He sat stretched out in the back seat while Tessa sat with Serge in the front, waving goodbye to the officer and the nurse.

Tessa noticed that for once Serge drove with particular care.

Alex was quiet on the way back as he listened to Tessa's account of what had happened.

"That's someone who will never work with us again," Alex said. "It was my father and Weber's father who started the firm years ago making plastic kitchenware. Later, when we both inherited the firm, we realised that what people wanted was not just gadgets but something that actually helped them with the chores. That's when we started thinking about domestic robots. A contact of Weber's got to know about this, and we were offered a military contract to design and build peacekeeping robots. That is why we have a research centre on the top of a mountain. It was important to keep that aspect of our work separate."

"But what about Weber? As I told you, he escaped with a formula for the plastic that didn't work. Won't he come back to bother us again?" Tessa was still worried.

"The police will be onto him, so don't worry." Alex reassured her.

They arrived at Alex's chateau, and as they helped him up the short flight of steps to the front door, it opened and Maria came flying out.

"I saw you arrive from the window," she said. "What's happened?"

Tessa took in the slender young form, the golden hair, blue eyes open wide as in shock, and felt a pang of jealousy.

"I'm fine, "Alex said, limping between Tessa and Serge. "Just a little skiing accident. I'll tell you all about it later."

Safely settled in a chair by a roaring fire with Maria fussing over him, he held Tessa's hand. "Thank you for everything, both of you. I'll be mobile soon and we'll sort this out."

"Would you like me to stay?" Tessa asked.

"No, I'll be fine, Maria will look after me."

Tessa felt as though she had taken a physical blow. *I'm right, he doesn't really care about me at all. Well, in that case . . .*

They waved goodbye and Serge took Tessa back to her hotel.

"That was exciting," Serge said, "Ana and Hans are back together again. I wonder how long it will be before they can get off the mountain?"

"Not long, I should think, now that the police are aware of the situation." Then a thought struck her. "What about the robots that Weber sent to guard us? They are still up there waiting for orders."

"I'm sure the staff can cope with that, and once the phone lines are working again, Alex can deal with any problems. You could phone him and remind him if you like, but I'm sure he's thought of it." Serge suddenly went all shy. "And can I see you again soon?" he asked.

Tessa looked at him in a new light. He wasn't a young lad, he was a man, and a handsome one at that. She made a decision. "Dinner tonight, here in the hotel?" she asked, smiling.

"Thanks," he stammered. "What time?"

"About a quarter to eight should be fine. I'll meet you in the dining room."

Serge looked nervous. "And what should I wear?"

"Just something neat, you don't need to be formal."

He went away looking as though he had just won a prize.

Tessa collected her key from reception, went to her room and collapsed onto the bed.

"What a day," she murmured, "I think I'll just have a little rest."

She woke up with a start, looking at the bedside clock. It was six o'clock.

"Goodness, that was quite a sleep. I obviously needed it," she said. "Now a shower and change before I entertain Serge."

The Maître d' conducted her to her favourite table just as Serge came into the dining room. He waved as he walked across the room towards her.

Such a good looking young man. I haven't really taken much notice of him before.

He was dressed in a smart lounge suit, wearing a white shirt with open neck, no tie. He looked so different from the casually dressed person who had been with her on their dash to see Dr Faure.

A line from a Yip Harberg song ran through Tessa's mind, *When I'm not near the girl I love, I love the girl I'm near.*

Perhaps it works the other way round.

Serge looked around nervously as he sat down opposite her. "Do I look all right?" he asked.

"You're fine," Tessa reassured him. She guided him through the menu and they both settled on crab bisque, followed by sea bass.

"And for wine, monsieur?" The waiter looked at Serge, handing him the wine list.

"You choose." Serge passed it rapidly to Tessa.

Tessa smiled, pointing to Sauvignon Blanc. "A good wine, you'll enjoy it."

Serge gave the wine list back to the waiter. "That will be

fine. This is a real treat for me," he said, fiddling with his cut-lery.

"Oh, I don't know. I enjoyed our evening out at your local café very much. This is just a bit different."

Serge began to relax as the meal was served.

Tessa discovered to her surprise that he was interested in Swiss history and was able to tell her more about what she had missed in Bern.

"You should have climbed the spire of Berne' cathedral—the view over the city is stunning. On a clear day you can see all the way to the Eiger, Mönch and Jungfrau mountains."

"We saw the clock tower, but didn't go in to see the mechanism."

"You should have done. It's thirteenth century and has been a watch tower, a prison and now a famous clock."

Tessa felt relaxed in his company.

This is the second pleasant meal I've had with him. He really is a good companion, but I don't feel the attraction to him that I feel with Alex. I wonder why?

She looked at his face as he talked animatedly about the Switzerland he loved.

While he was talking she mentally compared him with Alex. They were so different, not only in age but in sophistication. Serge was so natural, whereas Alex, well Alex was just Alex.

She fell into a reminiscence where she and Alex were skiing down the mountain together and was brought up with a jolt with the waiter asking about the dessert.

Surprisingly, Serge took the lead on this one. Quickly scanning the menu he asked for chocolate mousse.

Tessa, a little slower, picked tarte tatin.

Afterwards in the lounge, they drank their coffee in comfortable silence.

Tessa stifled a yawn. "It's been a long day," she said. "I'm sorry, I must go up now and you must be tired."

Serge stood up as she rose. "I've had a wonderful and exciting day," he said. "Can I get in touch tomorrow?"

"Of course." Tessa went to shake hands and was alarmed when he pulled her to him, giving her a hug.

He made to kiss her, but she turned her face and put her hand to his lips.

"No, Serge. Don't spoil a perfect day." She turned away.

Serge looked confused and disappointed. "I thought—" He turned and almost ran out of the lounge.

Tessa went thoughtfully up to bed.

As she lay in the dark, her thoughts turned to Alex.

Why am I so attracted to him and not Serge? There must be some strange magic in the attraction between people. I'm sure Alex feels it too.

And with that she fell into a dreamless sleep.

Alex sat by the fire thinking about Tessa. He hadn't wanted to bother her with his troubles, but he really would have liked her to stay. His foot hurt as he moved it.

Maria came in. "Is there anything I can do for you?" she said, hovering in front of him.

"Stop fussing, girl," he snapped. "Your job is to look after Luka, not me. Ask Mrs Benson if she can prepare a cold supper for me. You had better eat with Luka in the usual way."

Maria shot out of the room as though she had been slapped in the face.

Mrs Benson, his housekeeper, came in. "You'll take your meal here?" she asked.

"Yes, Mrs Benson. I can hobble about with this stick." He waved it. "But I think I'll be more comfortable here than at the table."

Meal over, he sat looking into the fire. It had been long years since his wife had died, and he felt the need for a companion.

I am attracted to Tessa,. but I'm not sure that she even likes me.
And with that thought he struggled up to bed.

Next morning Tessa woke early, the sun flooding into the room. She rose, stretched, washed, dressed and went down to breakfast.

A phone call to Serge confirmed that communication had been re-established with the research centre, the lift was working again, and Hans and Ana were due to come down that morning.

"I'm going to Grindelwald to meet them," Serge said. "Do you want to come?"

"That would be great," Tessa said.

"I'll meet you at the hotel in an hour," he said. "If that's all right?"

Serge arrived dressed in a leather jacket and jeans.

Tessa met him in the lobby, and they set off for Grindelwald. Tessa noticed that after their experience the previous evening he made no attempt to kiss her as he helped her into the car.

"I'm not sure what time they will be down," he said as they drove off. "I told them I would meet them in the café."

The journey was uneventful, although with snow falling gently Serge took particular care with his driving.

Tessa sat quietly in the front with him, her thoughts still on Alex.

When they arrived at Grindelwald, Tessa went straight to the mountain rescue office while Serge was parking the car. The same officer was sitting at the reception desk, smoking. He stood up as she entered, stubbing his cigarette in the ash-tray.

"Welcome. How is your friend? You haven't come to re-port another accident I hope?"

"No, I just wanted to thank you and your nurse for the help

and kindness you gave us when Mr Baxter injured himself."

The officer motioned her to one of the two chairs in front of his desk.

"Can I get you something to drink?" He turned to the cupboard behind him.

"Thank you, but no, I must get back to my friend. I expect you have heard about what went on at the Roboplastix research centre?"

The officer smiled. "Yes, it was quite an exciting story. We had the local police chief in here yesterday. I believe they are hunting for a criminal called Weber."

"I just hope they catch him quickly," Tessa said with feeling. "He has caused enough trouble."

The officer leant forward and patted her arm. "Don't worry, my dear young lady, our police are very efficient. Goodbye and good luck."

"Thank you." Tessa waved as she walked out into the icy street. A horse drawn sled passed her as she made her way to the café where Serge was waiting.

After about half an hour, sitting in the café drinking coffee while Serge regaled her with more tales of his beloved Switzerland, the door opened, and there was Ana hanging on the arm of Hans, her face shining with happiness.

As they sat down, Tessa could see that Ana was bursting with news.

"Hans has asked me to marry him, and I've accepted." She looked across at Hans who leant over and patted her hand.

"We shall be married as soon as it can be arranged," he said.

"Congratulations." Tessa kissed Ana on the cheek.

Serge shook hands with Hans.

"Which church will you choose to be married at?" Tessa asked Ana.

Hans replied for her. "In Switzerland, it's a civil ceremony.

Yes, we could get married in church, but we don't have to. It's only legal when you get married in a registry office."

Tessa looked disappointed. "I was looking forward to seeing Ana dressed in a flowing white wedding dress coming down the aisle."

Ana smiled. "I can still have the wedding dress, but I won't be walking down the aisle."

"That's the other problem," Hans said. "Most of these registry offices are in old buildings, so we can't have very many guests. We shall have to hold another ceremony somewhere larger afterwards with more guests, but we want you, Tessa, and Serge to come to the registry office. We need two witnesses, if you would be willing?"

Tessa looked at Serge, who nodded. "We would be honoured," she said. "They obviously do things differently here."

Hans explained. "We have to present our birth certificates, passports and proof of identity. We even have to show our parents' family record document. It will take at least five weeks before we can have the ceremony."

"Will you be able to stay that long, Tessa?" Ana asked.

Tessa thought for a moment. "No, I shall have to go back to England, but let me know the date and I'll be back." Then turning to Hans, she asked, "What is a family record document?"

"It's a record of our parents' marriage and details of their children." Hans turned to Ana. "Do you have your document safe?"

Ana looked nervous. "I'm not sure if I have it. Both my parents are dead. I have a box of papers from them, but I haven't really looked through it properly."

Hans put his arm round her. "We'll look together."

They stood locked in each other's arms until Serge suggested that he should drive them all back to Zurich.

CHAPTER EIGHT

With Ana and Hans in the back seats and Tessa sitting next to him, Serge drove carefully as snow was beginning to fall again.

In the car Serge said quietly to Tessa, "I wish you weren't going. Do you have to go back to England? Can't you stay?"

"I wish I could, but my Head of Department will be worrying about me. I'll be back, never fear."

They dropped the two lovebirds at Ana's apartment. Hans was still holding Ana tight as they entered the apartment building.

Serge drove onto the Splendide, getting out and opening the car door for Tessa.

As she got out, he shook hands awkwardly.

"See you soon," she said and walked rapidly into the hotel without looking back.

Once in her room and checking her diary, she was surprised to see how quickly her time away from the department had passed and it was sad to think that she now should organise her return.

She put in a call to England, to the head of the Chemistry Department, Professor Tom Neally, at the University, to explain briefly all that had happened.

"I'll be back as soon as I can arrange a flight," she said.

"You do lead an interesting life." He laughed. "But it will be good to have you back."

After the phone call, Tessa sat back and reviewed all that had happened and what she must do before she left. She made a list on the small pad by her bed.

1. Phone Alex and tell him I shall be leaving for England but will be back for the wedding.

(I don't want to see him. That might cause further complications because of my feelings for him. Anyway he's got Maria)

2. Fix my flight, tomorrow if possible. (Good job I have an open ticket)

3. Ring Sandy to let her know I'm coming.

4. Pay my hotel bill.

5. ? Serge.

She sat back. *What to do about Serge? He is obviously attracted to me. I like him, but I don't have the same feeling for him as I do for Alex.*

She sighed, pushed her list away, rang the airline and was fortunate to be able to fix a flight for the next day. She spent the rest of the time before dinner, packing all but the essential things she would need.

Dinner was a lonely affair, but as soon as she got back to her room the phone rang, it was Serge.

"I just thought," he said. "When are you flying? I could give you a lift to the airport."

"That's kind of you," she said, thinking quickly. "I'm catching the afternoon flight tomorrow. I have to leave the hotel at two o'clock. Can you manage that?"

"I'll be there," he said, and Tessa detected a happy note in his voice.

Like all nights before travelling, Tessa slept badly. She had vivid dreams in which Alex and Serge were fighting a duel.

She woke up before she knew the outcome. The sun streamed in the window, and as she sat up in bed she realised that she hadn't phoned Alex. Making a mental note to do so after breakfast, she washed and dressed and went down, stopping at reception to explain that she was leaving that afternoon and paying her bill.

After breakfast she phoned Alex. "How are you?"

"I'm fine, I can hobble about a bit. Can you come over?"

Tessa took a deep breath. "No, sorry I'm going back to England this afternoon. I've fixed my flight."

She detected sadness in his voice. "I can't come to see you off," he said, "Could you come over to say goodbye? I shall miss you terribly."

"No, I have things to do but don't worry, I'm coming back in time for Hans and Ana's wedding in about five weeks' time and I'll see you then, I hope."

"They're getting married? Good for them."

Tessa expected him to say something about their own relationship, but he didn't.

That's it then, she thought, as she put the finishing touches to her packing.

Feeling sad, she went down the grand staircase to the lounge for a sandwich lunch.

She almost expected Alex to turn up. He kept turning up before, why not now?

She went back to her room and was just about to take her suitcase down when the phone rang. It was Serge waiting for her at reception.

Her suitcase was loaded into the boot, she got into the car, the concierge waved them off, and they were on their way to the airport. Serge parked the car and carried her case for her into the terminal. He stayed with her while she checked in, and as she was going through passport control, she could see he was hesitating on how to say goodbye. She leant forward while holding his hand and giving him a kiss on the cheek. Quickly she turned, waved goodbye, and was through passport control without looking back.

When she reached the departure lounge, she found that the plane was delayed by half an hour. She was sitting on a seat next to a young child and her mother. The child was complaining, "Why can't we go on the aeroplane now?"

The mother smiled at Tessa and looked down at her child playing with a small doll.

"It will be soon, Lena, play with Gertrude for a while and then we shall go."

The girl seemed satisfied with this and began to rearrange her doll's hair.

Tessa took out her book and settled down to read. That kept her occupied until the flight was called and the passengers all got up in a dash for the departure door. She got up slowly. There was no rush, as she had a numbered seat. It always amazed her that people were so nervous that they had to rush as though they would miss their plane if they didn't.

As she boarded the plane, she saw Lena and her mother sitting in one of the front seats.

Walking down the aisle she looked for her seat, 6A, a window seat and found a large woman sitting in it. She leant over to show the woman her ticket. "I think you're sitting in my seat," she said.

The woman took out her own ticket and looked at it. Then, grumbling to herself she got up, waddled into the aisle, and let Tess slide past her. When Tessa was safely seated she sat down next to her and immediately began to eat a chocolate bar. Once they were airborne the woman dropped the chocolate wrapper on the floor and immediately settled down and fell asleep.

Not exactly the companion I had last time, Tessa thought, immersing herself in her book.

The flight was uneventful. Getting her luggage at Heathrow took a while, but then she took a taxi back to her flat in Guildford.

As she walked up the stairs, her neighbour, Mrs

Farrington, opened her door. "Tessa, you're back."

"Hello Else, yes, I'm back for a while. What's been happening while I've been away?"

"Nothing much, my cat's had kittens. I've given most of them away, but I've got one left, if you would like it?"

Tessa laughed. "No thanks, I don't think Sandy would approve, she doesn't like cats."

"Oh, I know. I mentioned it to her the other day. Anyway, nothing much has happened except the butcher's run off with the local barmaid. We're going to have to get our meat from the supermarket. It's a shame all the local shops are closing."

"Thanks, Else, see you later." Tessa opened her door and went into the flat.

Sandy wouldn't be back from work for a while, so Tessa had the place to herself. She went to her room and started to unpack.

When Sandy arrived, she took one look at Tessa and said, "Well, how did the conference go? You've got that look in your eye. Did you meet someone?"

Tessa turned away to hide her confusion. "How did you know that?" she asked.

"Elementary my dear Watson," Sandy sat on the settee. "You're bound to meet someone on the rebound. Oh, I forgot to tell you, Rob came round the other day wanting to see you. I told him you were away and I didn't know when you would be back."

"Good," Tessa said. "I don't want to see him ever again, and yes, I did meet someone. I'll tell you all about it over dinner. Whose turn is it to make it?"

"Yours, of course, but as you're just back, I'll do it. I've got some nice chops for us. Did you hear about the butcher?"

"Yes, Else told me when I got here. So, no more meat locally?"

"Not true, the butcher's wife is going to keep the shop

going, she's found someone to help her. That's where I got the chops."

Tessa sat on the settee with her friend. "It's good to be back, I missed all the local gossip."

Sandy prepared the chops and served them with roast potatoes and broccoli. They celebrated Tessa's return with a bottle of red wine and finished the meal with tinned peaches and ice cream.

Afterwards, in bed, Tessa realised that she hadn't told Sandy about Alex. *I think I'll keep him a secret for now.*

Next day Tessa made her way to the university.

First, she reported to Professor Neally.

A big bear of a man, he rose from his chair. "Good to see you, I had a phone call from Dr Faure in Zurich. I gather you had quite an adventure with some sort of new plastic that he was telling me about."

"Yes, it was a bit hair raising at times, but it worked out all right in the end. I also met two characters who have designed a way of getting plastic waste out of our oceans. I attended a demonstration." She laughed. "I'm afraid I fell in the water, but that's another story."

Professor Neally looked concerned. "Were you all right? The water in Switzerland is a bit cold at this time of year."

"No, I was fine. I got rescued by some locals."

"Well, I'm glad you're back. You've had a Mr Fred Jackson trying to reach you."

"That's one of the men I told you about. Did he leave a phone number?"

"Yes, here it is." Neally handed her a memo slip. "Now, I expect you'll want to get back in harness."

"Thanks, yes I do, see you later."

She left his office, clutching the paper, and made her way to the office she shared with Edwin, an earnest young researcher who was her assistant.

He looked up as she came in. "Hi, Tessa, you're back then. How was the trip?"

"Good," she said, settling into her chair. "I ought to have phoned you, but things were a bit hectic. I'm writing a report so you can read all about it later. How have things been going at this end?"

Edwin turned in his seat. "Ticking along slowly," he said. "You had someone called Rob trying to contact you, but he didn't leave a message."

"Thanks Edwin, I'll deal with that." She looked at the mass of papers in her in tray.

"I suppose I'd better tackle this lot before I look at my emails." She sighed.

Tessa immersed herself in her work. She made contact with Fred, who invited her to his home. There she met his wife Angie and their two very well-behaved children, but she found that she was missing Alex terribly. Work helped, but when she was on her own in the flat her thoughts always came back to him.

Why doesn't he get in touch? I felt we were getting so close but now he seems to have shut me out. Should I phone him? No, five weeks is a long time, he'll have forgotten all about me. I must forget him.

Gradually she calmed down, but always at the back of her mind was that feeling of loss. She had an email from Ana telling her that the wedding was scheduled for the 24th of the month.

She replied, "I'll be there. Good luck."

If she was honest with herself, she was counting the days to when she would be back in Zurich for the wedding. Was it the wedding or the chance she might see Alex again?

Life continued peaceably and the days ticked away but with no contact from Alex, until one Saturday afternoon she got a phone call at the flat.

"Hi, Tessa, it's Serge. I'm at Heathrow. Just landed. This is a surprise visit. Can I come over?"

"Serge, what on earth are you doing in England?"

"I came to see you," he said simply.

"You mean you came all this way without telling me?"

"I had to," he said. "I realised I missed you so much. I had to come."

Tessa was taken aback. What should she do — what could she do?

"Look Serge, I don't have a car, so I can't pick you up. Do you have money for a taxi? You do? Right. Just get a taxi from the airport and come to my flat." She gave him the address.

Tessa put the phone down and staggered over to the sofa. She put her head in her hands. *What on earth has made him come over and what am I going to do with him?*

While she was still recovering, Sandy came in.

"What's happened? You look as though you've seen a ghost."

"In a way I have," she said, sitting up. "I've just had a phone call from a young man who helped us in Zurich. He's at Heathrow and says he's come to see me." She looked up at Sandy in anguish.

"You must have made quite an impression on him." Sandy sat by her.

"Don't joke. What am I going to do?"

"Well, he can't stay here," Sandy said. "You're going to have to send him home or at least find him somewhere to stay for the night. Is this a love match?"

"Oh, Sandy, nothing of the kind. He's just a young, deluded boy."

"Ho, ho, the plot thickens."

"No, it's nothing like that. I don't know what he's got into his head. He's a nice boy, but there was actually someone else I liked. Trouble is, I haven't heard from that one, so I suppose that's all over."

"Sounds as if you had a gay old time while you were in Switzerland."

"Never mind that. What am I going to do?"

"Whatever you do, be kind to the lad. If he thinks he's in love with you, treat him gently, then send him home."

Time passed. The doorbell rang, and Serge came in, carrying a suitcase.

"Hi, Tessa. Boy, Heathrow was crowded, I thought I'd never get a cab." He stepped forward and kissed her on the cheek.

"Come in, Serge, meet my flatmate, Sandy."

Sandy came forward and shook hands. Tessa could see Sandy weighing him up.

Serge put his case down and turned to Tessa, "Well here I am. Are you pleased to see me?"

"Of course, Serge, it was just a bit of a shock," Tessa said. "Why have you really come?"

"I told you," he said. "I realised how much you meant to me, so I just had to come and be with you."

"That's all very nice, but how about Hans and all the work you've been doing there?"

Serge wriggled uncomfortably. "Hans is a different person," he said. "All the time he's with Ana he doesn't seem to be able to settle to work, so I thought the best thing to do was to come and see you."

"It does give us a bit of a problem. Where are you going to stay, and how long do you want to be here for?"

Serge stood for a moment, thinking. "I'm sorry if this bothers you. I thought I might stay here with you. I didn't know you shared an apartment. Don't worry, I'll find somewhere."

"There's a bed and breakfast place in the next street. I pass the sign every morning when I go to work. Why not try there?" Sandy suggested.

"That's it then." Serge picked up his case, he looked sad. "I'll go there and go back home tomorrow."

"No, don't be hasty." Tessa felt guilty. "Sure, go and get yourself a bed for the night, but we'll give you a meal here tonight, won't we, Sandy?" She turned to her friend for reassurance. "And then tomorrow, Sunday, perhaps you would like to see some of the sights of London? You could go back on Monday?"

Serge said abruptly. "That's fine. Now how do I find this place where I can stay?"

"I'll take you." Sandy got up. "Won't be long, Tessa."

"Come back when you've settled in, Serge," Tessa waved.

When Sandy returned, she said, "Nice lad, but you obviously don't fancy him." She flopped down on the sofa. "Anyway, Mrs Stimson fixed him up with a room. I left him settling in."

"Yes, he is a nice lad, but what on earth possessed him to come to England?"

"He told us, he fancies you."

"Rubbish, that's just silly. By the way, I realised afterwards that I promised to show him some of the sights without thinking, but it's your car. Do you mind?"

"Of course not," Sandy said, stretching her feet out on the sofa. "What do you think we should show him?"

"More immediate problem," Tessa said. "What are we going to give him to eat? I bought just two pieces of salmon for tonight's meal."

"Easy," Sandy said. "We'll make a kedgeree."

"I'm impressed," Tessa said. "How do you do that?"

"It's easy," Sandy said. "Long grained rice, hard boiled eggs, your salmon, I'll show you. It will certainly stretch for three."

Serge arrived back at about seven o'clock looking more

cheerful.

"Nice lady," he said. "I'm booked in for bed and breakfast. I told her you were giving me dinner."

"Well, sit down, watch television if you like. We can talk about tomorrow after dinner." Tessa switched on the set, giving him the remote control, then went into the kitchen where Sandy was already at work.

"Thanks," Serge called.

When Tessa returned to lay the table, she found Serge watching motor racing. He looked up as she came in.

"I know what I want to do," he said, "I've just been watching motor racing from Brands Hatch. This is what I'm really interested in. I'm going to find a club, see if I can get a job in the sport."

"Why can't you do it in Switzerland?" Tessa asked.

Serge looked at her. "Don't you know, the Swiss Government is against it. It was banned in Switzerland after a bad crash at Le Mans in nineteen fifty-five. They are coming round a bit now, but it's still limited. Your country is the best. If I could get an apprenticeship or become a marshal. I told you when we met, I wanted to get into motor racing."

"Good for you," Tessa said. "We'll have a look on the web and see what the possibilities are, if that's what you really want."

"And it means I don't have to go back to Switzerland." Serge looked sideways at her.

"We'll have to check the regulations about living in this country, but let's do all that tomorrow." Tessa looked thoughtful. *This is going to be more complicated than I thought.*

Sandy brought the kedgeree in, and they had a pleasant meal together. Afterwards Serge left to go to his bed and breakfast place.

While they were piling the dishes into the dishwasher, Tessa said. "I don't think we're going to get Serge back to

Switzerland. He's told me he wants to live in this country and get a job in motor racing."

Sandy threw up her hands. "You're stuck with him?"

"Not necessarily, tomorrow I'll find out what the regulations are for him staying in this country and what jobs might be around. We might find he can't stay."

Next morning, Tessa found out that Swiss nationals could stay in England, and when Serge arrived, she was already looking on the web for jobs in motor racing.

"It looks as if you can stay with no problem," she told him, "but the jobs in motor racing seem to be specialised. Your best bet seems to be to get an apprenticeship with one of the motor clubs. You'll have to explore further."

"Mrs Stimpson, that's the lady I'm staying with, says I can stay on with her and she's given me a special rate if I will help her with some of the chores." Serge sprawled on the sofa.

"That's good news, but don't forget we have to go back for Ana and Hans's wedding in two weeks' time on the twenty fourth. We promised to be their witnesses."

Serge clapped his hand to his head. "Gosh, I had forgotten. At least I've got time to do some exploring, find out if it is possible to get into motor racing."

"Well, today Sandy and I are going to show you some of the sights of London. Have you had breakfast?"

"Yes, I have, thanks. Where are you taking me?"

Sandy came in at that moment. "Tower of London, although we won't let them keep you, the London Eye, and anything else you would like to see."

"How about Big Ben, the Houses of Parliament and Trafalgar Square?" Serge looked keen.

"I think we can manage that. Are you ready to go?"

Sandy's car was an old Fiat 500. "Small but convenient for London and for parking" she said as they all squashed in and she drove away.

Tessa had made a picnic, they did the sights, had their picnic in Regents Park and in the late afternoon made their way back to the flat.

"I won't stay," Serge said. "I've had a terrific day, thanks, but if I'm going to stay in this country, I've got to make my own way." He looked sadly at Tessa. "It's strange how things turn out, you plan one thing and it turns out to be something else."

"Stay and eat with us." Tessa still felt guilty.

"Thanks, but Mrs Stimson is giving me what she calls supper tonight and then tomorrow I've got to go job hunting. She says she'll let me use her computer."

"Let us know how you get on, and don't forget to contact me so that we can go to Zurich together on the twenty fourth."

When Serge had left Tessa flung herself on to the sofa and said to Sandy. "I felt terrible about that. I feel as though I've abandoned him."

"Don't worry," Sandy said. "He's a capable lad, and he's got to find his own way."

"I suppose you're right. It seems my two men from Switzerland have just left me."

"You haven't spoken much about the other one lately. I thought you were quite involved with him?"

"Alex, you mean. I thought so too, but three weeks and I haven't heard from him. He obviously wasn't as keen as I was."

Sandy put her arm round her friend's shoulder. "Someone else will come along, you'll see."

Next day someone did come along but it gave Tessa a shock. Serge had just come over in the evening to tell them he had been investigating jobs when there was a knock at the door. Sandy went to answer it.

She came back into the room, with a strange look on her face. "It's Rob," she said as he pushed past her, a tall gangly character advancing towards Tessa.

Tessa was sitting on the sofa with Serge. They were deep in conversation.

Tessa looked up in shock. "Rob, what are you doing here?"

"I've been trying to get to see you for ages," he said, then seeing Serge, he stopped suddenly.

"I've told you I don't want to see you again," Tessa was shaking.

"I just wanted . . ."

"It doesn't matter what you wanted. Get out of our flat and out of my life."

Serge looked startled by the abrupt change in Tessa's manner.

"What's all this?" he asked, getting up.

"None of your business, sonny," Rob gave him a push that sent him reeling back onto the sofa.

"Rob, stop that and leave now." Tessa stamped her foot.

"Do you want me to hit him?" Serge asked, getting up again, clenching his fists.

"No, Serge, this is an old boyfriend who won't take no for an answer. Go away Rob."

Rob looked uncertain as Serge took a step towards him. Then, muttering under his breath, he turned and walked out, slamming the door.

Tessa breathed a sigh of relief. "Thanks Serge, that was unfortunate, but I don't think he will trouble me again." She laughed. "I think he thought you were my new boyfriend."

"I wish I was," Serge said.

"Sorry, Serge, that was thoughtless of me. You are a very dear friend, but there is someone else."

Two weeks went by quickly. Ana sent emails confirming that

the wedding was still on for the 24th.

"You're off again," Sandy said.

"Yes, the wedding's next week. I've booked a morning flight for Serge and myself. We fly on the twenty first. He seems determined to make a go of it over here. I'm impressed, he's on some sort of training scheme with a motor club and seems happy enough. So we'll be back in three days' time."

"Well, good luck. I suppose you'll be seeing your friend Alex?"

"Depends, I'm not sure. I suppose if he's at the wedding I shall." Tessa turned away to hide her feelings.

On the morning of the 21st, Tessa met Serge at the airport. Serge now treated her like an older sister, for which she was grateful. The flight was on time. On the plane, Serge sat next to her telling her about the training scheme he had enrolled in.

Ana had arranged to meet them off the flight, but when they went through the *nothing to declare* exit and out into the main terminal there was no sign of her.

"I can't think what's happened." Tessa turned to Serge. "The last email I had said she would be meeting us."

"Are you sure you gave her the right time?" Serge asked.

Tessa looked at her watch. "Pretty sure. In any case the plane was twenty minutes late, so she should be here."

She looked again at the crowd of people waiting at the barrier. No familiar face.

"Now what do we do?"

Suddenly there was a shout, a man came from the left, waving.

Tessa felt her heart lurch. "It's Alex. What is he doing here?"

Alex ploughed through the crowd, coming up to them. "Sorry I was late, we got the time wrong."

"What are you doing here Alex? We expected Ana."

Alex laughed. "As you can imagine, Ana is a bit busy at the moment, so she sent me." He gave Tessa a hug. "I've missed you so much," he said.

He shook hands with Serge, who was standing by looking annoyed.

"Good to see you both again. Come on, I've got the car waiting."

They went to the car. Tessa noticed that he walked with a slight limp.

Stephan was in the driving seat, as usual, wearing his chauffeur's cap.

They got in, Alex ushering Serge into the front seat so that he could sit in the back with Tessa.

Alex reached across and held her hand. but Tessa couldn't help thinking. *If he missed me so much why didn't he keep in touch all these long weeks.*

As though he could read her thoughts, he said, " I'm sorry I haven't been in touch. I've been so busy these last few weeks. I know that isn't really an excuse, but we found out that Weber had been faking the books. He stole a lot of money, and there's been all sorts of complications. It's more or less sorted out now, thank goodness, but the police still haven't caught him. I was hoping to give you a surprise visit in England, but it wasn't possible. It's so good to see you." He gripped Tessa's hand firmly. "I'm taking you both to the chateau, I hope you'll both stay with me while you're here. Is that all right with you, Serge?"

Serge shook his head slightly. "I had thought to stay with Hans, but yes, thank you, it would be good to see how the boss of a big company lives."

Alex smiled.

Stephan swung the car into the driveway of the chateau and drove up to the house. They got out and walked up the steps to the front door, which was opened by Maria. Tessa saw Luka hiding behind her.

As they went in, Luka ran away.

"He's shy, isn't he?" Tessa said.

"He's always like this with new faces." Maria looked at Serge.

Tessa saw her look of interest. "Maria, let me introduce Serge.

Serge stepped forward and shook hands. Tessa noticed that he held on to her hand slightly longer than necessary while Maria looked at him, her eyes glistening.

Tessa smiled to herself as she watched them. *Perhaps this will deflect Serge's attention a bit from me?*

Maria seemed to realise what she was doing, releasing Serge's hand quickly and inviting them into the lounge, a large room with a bright log fire burning in the large fireplace.

Alex motioned them to sit down. "I don't know if you remember, Tessa, this house has a ballroom at the back where the family who owned it in the old days used to entertain. I've talked to Hans and Ana, and they have agreed to let me organise a reception for them there after the wedding, as Hans tells me there isn't much room in these old registry offices. We've sent invitations out already and of course you two as witnesses will be coming."

"That sounds great. And, yes, I do remember walking through that room on my disastrous visit."

Alex went over to her and put his hand lightly on her shoulder. "I know, I felt terrible about that, but it's all cleared up now, isn't it?" He looked at her as though needing reassurance.

She patted his hand. "Of course, you don't need to worry."

"I expect you would both like to see your rooms, and settle in," Alex said. "Maria, would you show them where they are?

Serge was looking about him in wonder and as they went up the broad staircase he whispered to Tessa, "I had no idea it would be as grand as this."

Maria obviously heard him and smiled.

Tessa was shown her room, the Royal suite.

"Ah yes, I remember this room, a four-poster bed," she said as she walked in.

Maria left her at the door and guided Serge along the corridor to a room three doors down.

Tessa did her usual bouncing on the bed and checking the pillows.

Even better than the Splendide, she thought, walking into the adjoining bathroom with its gold taps and large bath.

She had a quick wash then thought she ought to phone Ana to let her know they had arrived safely. She switched on her mobile but there was no signal.

Bother, I'll have to ask Alex if I can use his landline.

She went out onto the landing. As she did so, Maria came out of Serge's room, her face flushed, her eyes sparkling.

CHAPTER NINE

Without comment, Tessa went down the stairs to the lounge where Alex was standing warming himself in front of the fire.

"Alex, I can't get a mobile signal, can I use your phone? I want to let Ana know we've arrived."

"Of course," he said, pulling her to him and lightly caressing her back.

The feeling was so intense that she nestled forward into his arms and their lips touched. Maria came into the room, took one look and was about to walk out when Alex called, "Maria, can you show Tessa where the phone is? She wants to make a call." Alex stood back. "For some reason we can't get a mobile signal in the house. If you want to go down by the stream you might get one. But help yourself, there's a phone in the hall, Maria will show you."

"That's fine, it's just to tell Ana we're here."

Maria took Tessa into the hall and showed her the phone. Tessa dialled Ana's number. It rang and rang, but no-one answered. She dialled again but still no answer.

She went back into the lounge. "I can't get a reply," she said in a worried tone.

"She's probably out or over at Hans's place. I spoke to her this morning when we arranged that I should pick you up," Alex said, reaching out to her.

"Do you have Hans's number?" Tessa asked as he held her hands in his.

"It's in the phone book, I'll find it for you." Reluctantly he

146

released her hands. Going over to a side table he opened the phone book, flipping through the pages. "Here it is." He handed the book to her, pointing at the entry.

She took the book into the hall and got straight through to Hans, but he didn't know where Ana was.

"She should be at home," he said. "I spoke to her this morning, and we arranged to meet this afternoon."

"She's probably out shopping." Tessa bit her lip.

"I'm going over soon, so I don't think she'll be long as she knows I'm coming."

"I'll try again later but if you get there first, tell her we've arrived safely and will see her soon." Tessa put the phone down and went back into the lounge. "I can't get hold of Ana. She's probably just out. I'll try again a bit later. I spoke to Hans, so he'll tell her when he goes over."

"How about a walk in the garden while you're waiting to phone?" Alex looked quizzically at her.

Tessa thought for a moment, remembering the last time they had walked in the garden with such disastrous consequences.

"Yes, all right provided, Luka doesn't dash up to you and call you *daddy*." She grinned.

"Luka and Maria are safely tucked away in Luka's room. I think Serge may have gone to join them." He chuckled. "Maria seems to have made quite a hit with Serge."

Tessa smiled. "I noticed that as soon as Serge met her. Another budding romance?"

"How many do you want?" Alex caught her hand. "Come, put on a warm coat. It's gone colder since you were last here."

Tessa went quickly up to her room to collect her coat, hat, scarf and gloves.

Alex was waiting at the bottom of the stairs for her, clad in a heavy topcoat.

As she came down the last two steps he lifted her easily,

kissing her passionately.

Eyes closed, she surrendered to his lips.

"I've wanted to do that for a long time," he said. "Do you really want to go for a walk?"

Tessa stood back and looked at him smiling. "Of course I do, come on, a walk in the cold air will do you good."

"I know what would do me more good," he said, embracing her.

Shaking herself free, she held his hand. "Come on, let's go for this walk, and then I must make my phone call."

They walked through the old ballroom, on to the terrace and down into the garden. There was snow everywhere, but a path to the stream had been cleared. The water was still flowing sluggishly. They continued to hold hands while walking in companionable silence. There was no need for words.

Tessa turned to look at him. *I'm in love with this man, and I believe he is in love with me.* As they walked on, she felt a deep contentment. Alex squeezed her hand as though he too was thinking the same thoughts.

Tessa glanced at her watch. "Heavens, I was going to phone Ana. Look at the time, half an hour has gone by. She looked into his eyes. "That's what you do to me. Come on, we must go back."

Reluctantly Alex turned and led her back towards the house.

Even before taking her coat off, Tessa phoned Ana's number. "Still no reply," she said to Alex who was standing by her.

"Do you have her mobile number?" he asked.

"Yes, I do. It's upstairs in my diary. I'll go and get it."

He helped her off with her coat, putting it with his in the alcove under the stairs as she ran lightly up the stairs to her room.

As she came back down, holding her diary, sounds of merriment came from a room at the end of the top corridor.

Alex was still in the hall waiting for her as she phoned again, using Ana's mobile number.

"Still no answer," she said, turning to Alex. "She should be back by now. Hans said he was going over to see her. What can have happened?"

"I don't know. Why don't you go over to her apartment? Do you want me to come with you? We can go in my car. Stephan will drive us."

"It's kind of you to offer but you must have a million things you need to do." She looked at him with loving eyes. "There's no need to come with me, but I would like to go over to see if she is all right."

"I'll get Stephan to bring the car round for you. Hang on a minute."

At that moment Serge came bounding down the stairs and into the hall. "We've been having so much fun," he said, "Maria, Luka and me. He's a nice boy." He turned to Tessa who was looking anxious, "What's wrong?"

"I can't raise Ana on the phone, so I'm going over to see her."

"I'll come too," he said. "It's a pity I haven't got my car. I put it in my brother's garage before I left for England."

Alex came back. "Stephan's bringing the car round for you. I'll come if you like?"

Tessa went up to him. "Thank you, but you really don't need to, Serge will come with me. We shouldn't be long."

Stephan arrived at the front door and soon they were speeding to Ana's apartment block.

Tessa and Serge went up in the lift to Ana's second floor apartment.

Serge knocked at the door. "That's strange," he said as the

door swung open. "She would never leave her door open especially after the fright she had when her doll was stolen."

Tessa turned pale, clutching at Serge's arm as they went in.

The apartment had been wrecked. It was obvious that there had been a fight. Chairs overturned, a lamp smashed on the floor.

Tessa ran quickly to the kitchen, then the bathroom. No sign of Ana. She came back and leant against the table.

"What can have happened?" Her voice sounded shrill and unnatural.

Serge had been looking round, putting the furniture back, tidying up.

The phone rang. Tessa picked it up. It was a voice that she recognised. She put her hand over the receiver. "It's Weber," she whispered. "What do you want?" she said into the phone.

"It's not what I want, it's what you want," he said. "I've got your Ana, and if you want her back you'll have to exchange her for the plastic formula. I've been tricked once. I won't be again. I'll call again to give you further instructions. Don't contact the police." The phone went dead.

"What happened?" Serge asked, coming over to Tessa, who was trembling.

"Weber's got Ana and wants to exchange her for the plastics formula," she cried.

"Not again. Is that louse still at large? I thought we had got rid of him."

Suddenly Hans was in the room. "What's happened?" He glanced around the wrecked apartment. "Where's Ana?"

Tessa ran to him. "She's been kidnapped by Weber. He wants the formula."

Hans looked shattered. "We're to be married in two days' time. What can we do?"

"He said not to contact the police and he will phone with instructions." Tessa sat down in despair.

Hans seemed devastated by what had happened. "I must get in touch with Faure," he said. "He will have to give me the formula. I must get Ana back."

"I think we ought to contact Alex. After all, he is Weber's partner. He may know where he's hiding out," Tessa said. "You shouldn't give in so easily."

"I think Tessa's right." Serge went over to Hans. "We'll get her back, don't worry."

"Let's talk to Alex and see what he suggests. One of us had better stay here for Weber's next phone call."

"I'll stay." Hans volunteered. "The least I can do for Ana is to put this place straight. I'll call you as soon as I get any news."

"Call my mobile. Oh, no, Alex's place doesn't get a signal. What's his phone number?"

"Don't worry, I can look it up. You two get going." Hans started to pick up the furniture.

Stephan was waiting for them in the car, and they were soon back at the chateau.

Maria let them in, flashing a smile at Serge.

Alex was still in the lounge. He listened to what Tessa had to say, then opened a drawer, taking out a card. "Here's Weber's home address. He wouldn't dare go up the mountain again, so I assume he will have taken Ana here." He held out the card to Tessa.

"What do you think we should do?" she asked.

"Well, we can't go to the police, that's obvious. Let's go and catch him. We could hand him over to the police afterwards."

Tessa looked admiringly at Alex, "I didn't know you were such a hero," she said.

"Alex is right. I'm all for a fight." Serge swung a fist at an imaginary enemy.

"I think we should wait until he rings again," Tessa said.

"If Weber is careless, Hans will be able to trace the number he's ringing from."

"Good thinking, when do you think he'll phone?" As Alex spoke, the phone rang. It was Hans.

"He's just phoned and given us twenty-four hours to deliver the formula. He says he'll ring again to fix the rendezvous point."

Alex held the phone from his ear and relayed the information. "Do you want to speak to him."

Tessa took the phone. "Hans, it's Tessa. Listen, can you get the number of the call?"

"I can try. I'll call you back."

Two minutes passed and the phone rang. "I've checked the number, it's a mobile. I can give you the number if you like."

Tessa looked disappointed. "No. don't bother. Hang on to it. We had hoped it would be his home number so we would know where they had taken Ana."

"No such luck. He's obviously cleverer than that. Do you want me to stay here?"

"I don't think he will phone again today, so please yourself, but keep in contact with us. Use Alex's home number."

"I think I'll stay just in case she does come back," he said. Tessa detected desperation in his voice.

Putting the phone down, she turned to Alex. "No luck on the number, I'm afraid he was using a mobile."

"That probably means he has taken her to his house. He wouldn't want to give the game away by using his landline. The house is in the old part of town. Let's go and see if he's there."

They all piled into the car, Stephan driving.

As they rode through the busy streets Alex explained that Weber had a house down by the river.

They arrived in a quiet street, and Stephan parked the car away from the house.

"How do you think we should play this?" Tessa whispered.

"Frontal approach, I think," Alex whispered back.

"Why are you two whispering?" Serge said with a laugh. "Come on, let's go and ring the doorbell."

The house was set in a small garden with lawn and flower-beds which were obviously neglected.

Ringing the doorbell produced no results.

"We can't break the door down, can we?" Tessa looked at Alex. He shook his head.

"I'm all in favour of that," Serge said enthusiastically. "But no, I'll go round the back, there may be a window open." He set off along the narrow path skirting the house.

Tessa and Alex stayed by the front door until Serge appeared from inside, opening the door.

"There doesn't seem to be anyone about," he said, letting them in. He looked guilty. "I had to smash a window to get in. You'd have thought that would disturb anyone if they were in here."

"As long as it didn't disturb the neighbours," Tessa said as they walked through the unlit hall. "Your Weber doesn't seem to have been very house proud," she said, looking at the drab wallpaper.

"He's a very strange person," said Alex, opening doors and looking into rooms as they walked towards the stairs. "I've never liked him, but until now he seemed to be doing a good job. Now of course we have found out he's been fiddling the books."

Meanwhile Serge had bounded up the stairs. "There's no-one up here," he called. "Come and look at this."

They found him in a bedroom at the end of the landing with the light on.

"Look here," he said, as they entered. The window had been blacked out, the single bed had obviously been slept in as the sheets on the bed were crumpled and the pillow indented. He held up some lengths of cord that had been attached to the framework of the bed. "Someone has been kept a prisoner here," he said as Alex prowled around the room.

After going downstairs, they looked in the kitchen where they found the remains of a meal for two.

"It looks as if Weber brought Ana here and then for some reason cleared out quickly, possibly knowing that I would think of this place." Alex picked up a plate with a piece of bread on it.

"So, what do we do now?" Tessa asked.

"It looks pretty hopeless." Alex looked around. "We can search the place for clues, but I doubt if we shall find anything."

"He could be anywhere, and what about poor Ana?" Tessa shuddered.

They took a careful look round but there was nothing they could find that would help establish where Weber had gone.

"Get Faure's formula and give it to him," Serge said. "I vote we do that."

As they left the house, Alex looked thoughtful. "Yes, we must go and talk to Faure. Let's get over to the university and discuss it with him. We might be able to set a trap."

Faure was in his office, which was still untidy with books and papers.

"So this is the Alex you left in a snow drift," he said, getting to his feet and shaking hands.

"It was necessary to warn you about Weber, and at the time I couldn't make it, so Tessa came with Serge." Alex eyed Faure with awe. "Now this villain is resorting to kidnapping. We've been given twenty-four hours to exchange your formula for Ana." Alex glanced at his watch, "We spent some of that time hoping to corner Weber at his house. Although he had been there, he had obviously left hurriedly, taking Ana with him."

"The fake plastic formula obviously didn't stop him, and you now want me to give him the real one?" Faure dropped the ash from his cigarette onto his already messy desk.

"Not exactly." Tessa pushed books off a chair and sat down. Faure looked at her approvingly.

"So, what do you want?" he asked.

Tessa looked up at Alex. "I think the idea is to set a trap using your formula as bait. He will want us to take it to some meeting place, but if we could lure him back here, we might be able to trap him."

"Hmm, that might be possible, but you'll have to be pretty convincing, young woman." Faure looked at the others. "How do you intend to set about it?"

They spent some time discussing possibilities and it was agreed that when Weber made his final demand, setting up the meeting place, Tessa would persuade him to come to the university to collect the formula. They would make sure this time that he couldn't get out of the building by briefing the security guards.

"He won't do it, you know." Serge shook his head when they were in the car heading back to Ana's apartment.

"I'll try my best to persuade him," Tessa said. "Leave me at the apartment, I can relieve Hans, he needs a rest anyway. I'll sleep there tonight, then when Weber rings I'll take the call, persuade him to come to Faure, and you will have set the trap."

"I can't let you do that." Alex sounded concerned. "I'm going to stay with you."

They arrived at the apartment. Hans and Serge also protested that they ought to stay there, but were eventually persuaded to leave.

Tessa and Alex, on their own in the apartment, checked the

kitchen for food. There was enough to last them for a good few days. Then Tessa went into Ana's bedroom where her collection of dolls sat quietly on the side, including Hans's two dolls. Alex followed her in.

"That's funny," Tessa said. "Why did Weber snatch Ana and leave the dolls? I suppose maybe finding that he couldn't analyse the plastic, he didn't bother to take them."

"That's probably true." Alex picked one of the dolls up, marvelling again at the flexibility of the plastic covering.

"We must find Ana," Tessa said, desperately sitting down on the bed.

Alex sat by her side and put his arm around her. "We will, don't worry. In the meantime let's go back to where we were once before."

She snuggled up to him as she felt the top button of her blouse being undone and clutched him tighter.

"Shouldn't we be listening for the phone," she said, as his hands caressed her body.

He smiled and undid another button. Wild excitement claimed her as he gently undid her blouse and eased it off her shoulders.

Her whole body felt alive as he reached round and undid her bra. He stripped off his shirt and she felt his ripping muscles as he slid her slacks down revealing her briefs.

As he took them off, he divested himself of the remainder of his clothes, and their naked bodies entwined. This time there was no hesitation as he slid a condom over his hard penis, his hands teasingly on her breasts, his lips on hers. Tessa felt his hands gradually caressing her lower and lower. Her body arched in anticipation.

"Yes, yes," she breathed, scarcely aware of what she was saying as he entered her.

They came together and an intense orgasm rippled through her body. As they lay together afterward, she found herself drifting off to sleep.

When she came to, she found that Alex has already show-ered and was dressed.

"Come on, lazy bones." He pulled her out from under the sheets. After a long kiss Tessa went to the bathroom and showered. After dressing, she went into the kitchen to pre-pare an omelette. The phone rang. She rushed to it and picked it up. It was Weber.

"Who is this and have you got the formula?" he asked.

"I'm Tessa Corston, Ana's friend and no, we haven't got the formula. Dr Faure won't let us have it, but he has agreed to release it to you in exchange for Ana. Go to Dr Faure's office as before."

"Do you think I'm crazy?" Weber said. "I'm not going to get caught in a trap. You will bring the formula to me."

Tessa made her voice sound desperate. "We can't, Dr Faure will only release it to you at his laboratory."

"Hard luck," Weber said, a note of triumph in his voice. "I'll give you until six o'clock tonight when it's dark. Meet me in the middle of the Quaibrucke, that's the Quay bridge in English. It's over the River Limmat, just on the outflow of Lake Zurich. Bring the formula. Come alone, or Ana goes in the water. The way I've tied her up, she won't be able to swim. No tricks."

"Wait!" Tessa yelled, but the phone went dead. "He didn't fall for it," she told Alex. "He wants me to bring the formula to the Quaibrucke over the Limmat at six o'clock tonight. What should we do?"

"I know the bridge, the water is pretty deep and nasty just there. I'll contact Faure and explain the position. I'll ring Stephan and get him to pick us up. As Hans and Serge are at the chateau, we can have a council of war. I'll give them a ring and let them know what has happened."

Stephan arrived and they were soon back in the chateau.

As they walked into the hall, Alex embraced her.
Hans came out to greet them.
Tessa gently disengaged herself from Alex.
"Don't mind me," Hans said. "Come on in. Faure's on his way."
Serge stood up as they followed Hans into the lounge.
Hans said. "Let me fill you in on what's happened. After your phone call, I contacted Faure, and he has agreed to make up another fake formula and bring it over."
"Surely Weber won't fall for that again," Tessa said.
"He won't get a chance," Serge said. "I'm going to be with you, and I shall rush him before he can do anything."
We also need a backup plan," Alex said. "Hans, if you will come with me, we can be in my boat under the bridge some time before six o'clock so that he won't know we're there, and if Ana does go into the water we will be able to pick her up. I'm a strong swimmer, so it will be easy for me to rescue her. Tessa, you go up to him with the package. Then if all goes well and he releases Ana, Serge will grab him and we'll turn him over to the police. If he does throw her into the water, that should be no problem."
Maria came in, followed by Dr Faure who was carrying a slim envelope. He looked even larger than Tessa remembered him as he ambled over to Alex, handing him the envelope.
"Here it is," he said, looking round for a seat. He knocked the ash off his cigarette into the fireplace and sat heavily on the only vacant chair near the fire, which creaked under his weight.
"Tessa, you had better have this," Alex said, handing her the envelope, then turning to Faure. "Tessa will deliver the package, and we think we've covered all angles. Thanks for your cooperation."

Faure threw his cigarette into the fire, where it drew everyone's attention by flaring up.

"Don't I get any fun out of this?" he rumbled.

"Join us on the yacht if you like," Alex said. "Can you swim?"

"Are you joking? I float like a porpoise. " He patted his ample tummy.

Mrs Benson, Alex's housekeeper and cook, served them sandwiches and fruit in the dining room.

After the meal Alex suggested they all take it easy until they should get ready for the evening.

"Come for a stroll by the stream again," he said to Tessa.

Hans was deep in conversation with Dr Faure, and Serge had gone out into the garden with Maria and Luka to play with the boy, making a snowman and throwing snowballs.

The sun shone in the clear blue sky. Tessa looked at Alex as they crossed the lawn onto the path by the stream. It felt good to be alive and with the man she now knew she loved. Then her thoughts turned to Ana. She clutched Alex's arm. "We must rescue Ana," she said.

"We shall, my love." Alex put his arm round her as they walked along the path. As they turned a corner out of sight of the others Alex pulled her to him.

Suddenly Luka came running up to them. "Daddy, Daddy, come and look." He dragged his father by the hand. They followed him back to the lawn, where Maria and Serge were looking down at a tiny hedgehog.

"Look Daddy, a hedgehog, it has lost its mummy."

Alex lifted it gently. "Let's put it under that bush. I'm sure it will find its way home."

He carried it over to the nearby bush and put it down carefully. As they watched, a tiny snout poked out from beneath its covering of spines and the tiny creature began to move farther under the bush.

"Let's leave it now," Alex said. "All back to the house."

Faure and Hans were still deep in conversation when they went in.

At four o'clock, Alex looked at his watch. "I've alerted my boat crew, but I must be there to make sure we get under the bridge well beforehand," he said. "The timing is going to be crucial. Tessa, are you sure you're all right with this?"

Tessa smiled, "It's a bit scary, but with Serge to back me up, I'll be fine."

"Hans, you'd better come with me now, we need to get the boat in position."

"I'll come too," Faure rumbled. "I want to see this."

Serge drove Tessa to near the bridge, parking in a side street. It was five minutes to six, and the light was failing as they approached the bridge.

"I'll stay out of sight until the last moment," he whispered. "Keep him talking as long as you can."

"I'll do my best," Tessa whispered back as she slipped out of the car, holding the envelope Faure had given her.

The six o'clock chimes rang out from a nearby church. As she walked onto the bridge she could just see a van parked in the middle of the bridge. It was getting really dark now and as she went towards the centre, she could hear the water rushing below. She looked over the low parapet. The water looked black and menacing. There was no sign of a boat. Had Alex been held up? It was too late to worry about that now.

As she reached the van, the back doors opened and a figure came out holding what looked like a large bundle, placing it on the parapet. Tessa thought that it must be Ana, bound and gagged. The bundle wriggled uncomfortably and tried to speak but the words were muffled.

Weber seemed larger than before, looming over Tessa, a menacing figure in the near dark. "Give me what you're holding," he said.

Tessa gave him the envelope.

Weber obviously didn't trust her. "I think I should see the contents of this envelope before we go any further. You tricked me once. You won't do it again."

He released his hold on Ana, who sagged near the edge of the parapet. Taking a torch from his pocket, he tried to tear open the envelope with one hand while holding the torch and the envelope in the other.

"Don't move," he said as Tessa took a step towards Ana, worried that she might topple over. He shone the torch in her face, momentarily blinding her.

The next second Serge, who had crept up behind him, knocked the torch out of his hand and seized him round the waist.

"Tessa, get Ana," he yelled as Weber struggled in his grasp.

Tessa ran towards Ana. Weber tore free from Serge, grasping Ana's small figure as Serge came back towards him.

Tessa grabbed Ana and tried to hold on to her. Serge and Weber fought as Tessa managed to pull Ana away.

Weber, with his superior strength, hoisted Serge onto the parapet, trying to throw him over. Serge pushed him back with all his might and then swung him round until Weber was balanced half over the parapet. Leaving Ana safe for the moment, Tessa jumped forward, grasped Weber's ankles and heaved. Their combined efforts resulted in Weber sliding forward, losing his balance and tumbling down into the dark water beneath with an almighty splash.

Almost immediately a boat came out from under the bridge shining a spotlight and Tessa could see a figure being hauled out and onto the desk of the boat.

Serge slid off the parapet. Tessa went back to Ana who had slumped onto the ground. Serge went into the van to switch on its headlights so they could see how Ana had been tied.

"This will hurt," Tessa said as she grasped the sticky tape over Ana's mouth and pulled gently.

"Ouch! Ouch!" Ana yelled.

"Sorry, let me untie you," Tessa said, reaching for the knots on Ana's tightly tied wrists. Then as she found it too difficult, "Serge, can you untie Ana for me?"

Still panting from his exertions, he helped Ana to the front of the van, so that he could see. Then, producing a Swiss Army knife, he cut the cords round her wrists.

"Thanks," Ana said, shaking with fear and rubbing her sore wrists. "I was so frightened. I can't believe I'm still alive."

Tessa held Ana in her arms, trying to calm her, then took her into the van and sat holding her hand.

Meanwhile, Serge leant over the parapet. "Did you get him?" he called down to the boat beneath,

"We got him all right. Thank goodness it wasn't Ana who fell in," Alex called back. "This time we'll hand him over to the police when we get ashore. See you back at the house." He waved as the boat drew away from the bridge. They could see Weber, a sodden bundle at Alex's feet.

CHAPTER TEN

Sometime later when they were all back at the chateau, Alex poured them a drink while they clustered round the fire to get warm. "The police have him this time. He won't bother us again."

"Alex, you should have seen the look on your face when you thought you were rescuing Ana, but Weber came out." Hans hugged Ana to him.

Alex laughed. "It was a bit of a shock, I must confess. We heard the splash and immediately brought the boat out from under the bridge. Our spotlight located the dark shape in the water. I jumped in to rescue, as I thought, a helpless Ana when what I actually found was a tough, fighting Weber. I must confess I had to hold his head under water until he stopped struggling, then we hauled him on board."

Faure went over to the fire, rubbing his hands together. "I don't think I've had so much fun in years. Obviously, working in a laboratory makes you get out of touch with the real world." He looked across at Hans, who was still hugging Ana.

Ana wriggled in Hans's arms. "The worst part for me was when Weber burst into my apartment. He carried me down to his van, his hand over my mouth to stop me screaming. I don't know where he took me, but after that he was quite courteous. Although what he would have done if you hadn't rescued me, I don't know."

"He was going to throw you in the water." Hans shuddered at the thought. "But you're all right now, and we're getting married the day after tomorrow. That is, if you feel up to it?"

Ana kissed him on the cheek. "Of course, but I don't want to stay alone in the apartment tonight, Tessa would you stay with me until the wedding?"

"Happy to." Tessa held Ana's hand. "But you've only got one bed?"

"Sleep in the bath." Serge laughed.

Tessa turned to him. "Have you ever tried that?"

"Never," he said. "I should think it's very uncomfortable."

"It is," said Alex, "I tried it when I was a student and wouldn't ever want to try it again. I'll get Mrs Benson to take the mattress off one of the spare beds upstairs. You can take it to the apartment and use it to sleep on the floor. Hans and Serge, you're welcome to continue staying with me until the wedding."

"Thanks," Hans said., "All right by you Serge?"

"Fine," he said. "I'm enjoying this life of luxury."

"What about me?" Faure said. "Can I come to the wedding as well?"

"Of course, but now you'll all be hungry, I'll see if Mrs Benson can rustle up a meal for us all."

"We ought to get going soon if we're to get back to Ana's place," Tessa said, turning to Alex. "Can you get the mattress? How can we get it in a taxi?"

"Don't worry about that. Have a meal first, then Stephan can drive you. We can put the mattress in the boot."

He turned to Faure. "After the meal, you're welcome to stay here if you wish."

Faure heaved his bulk out of his chair and stubbed his cigarette out onto the fireplace. "Thanks, I must get a taxi and go back to my place, but I will look forward to seeing you all at the reception."

The next day was spent getting Ana ready. She was

suffering from pre-wedding nerves and Tessa was pleased that she could be there to help.

Tessa phoned Professor Tom Neally, her Head of Department. She thought he didn't sound very happy at her wanting to stay in Zurich, but he gave her permission. "You know what you're doing. Just get back as soon as you can."

The wedding day dawned. Tessa looked out of the window at the mountains, shining white with snow, the sun glinting on them. It was a gorgeous day. She drew a deep breath. *Why couldn't this be me?*

Ana came into the room.

"You look wonderful." Tessa looked at Ana's slim figure dressed all in white. The fitted bodice made her waist so tiny, the long flowing skirt, the chantilly sleeves. It looked just right.

"I'm sure I've forgotten something," Ana said nervously.

"Nonsense," Tessa reassured her. "Everything will be fine."

Alex sent his chauffeur, Stephan, to pick them up.

Hans was already waiting in the registry office together with Serge.

It was a simple ceremony, Tessa and Serge acting as witnesses at the signing.

Ana looked radiant. Hans, dressed in a formal grey suit, couldn't take his eyes off her.

They walked together out of the registry office, holding hands, Tessa and Serge walking behind them.

The car was waiting to whisk them away to the reception at Alex's chateau.

When they got there they found the ballroom transformed with white draped hangings on the walls, magnificent crystal chandeliers lighting the scene. Guests were already waiting as Ana and Hans entered. Everyone clapped as the wedding march was played and the happy couple made their way to a table at the front of the room. As they did so, a small doll-like robot dressed as a maid came in from the side door bearing the cake, a three-tiered wedding cake with two tiny figures on the very top. It stopped in front of them as if uncertain what to do next.

Hans reached out and took the cake, placing it safely on the table.

"Aren't we supposed to cut it?" Ana asked, "But we can't cut all three layers."

Maria handed Ana a long-bladed knife. "Don't worry, I'll handle the top tiers, you just concentrate on the bottom one." She removed all but the lower layer, putting it on the plate the robot doll was holding.

The robot wheeled away and disappeared though the side door.

"Mrs Benson will cut slices for the guests, assuming that doll gets the cake to her." She smiled. "You two concentrate on cutting the cake."

In traditional fashion, Ana grasped the knife, Hans holding her hand. As they cut the cake together, a roar of approval went up from the guests with more clapping.

Maria quickly took the remainder of the cake out to Mrs Benson in the kitchen.

Alex was dispensing champagne to everyone. He brought glasses to Ana and Hans. Tessa was holding two glasses of champagne and handed one to Alex, who raised his glass. "To Ana and Hans for a lifetime of happiness and joy."

The toast was echoed by everyone present.

Two robot dolls came out, holding the cut pieces of cake on plates for people to take a piece.

"I thought they talked?" Tessa asked as she chose a slice.

"They do, but I thought it best not to let them do so on this occasion," Alex said, biting into his cake.

A buffet was then served on tables at the side and afterwards there was a display of national Swiss folk dances with three men and three women dressed in traditional costume, dancing to the music of a trio of musicians, one playing an accordion, another a fiddle and the third playing the hackbrett, a kind of zither.

"The strings are struck with small hammers," Alex explained to Tessa as the music went on. The dancers began to invite the guests to join in.

"It's a kind of formation dancing, as you can see. Come on, Tessa." He dragged her into the centre as some of the other guests took to the floor to join them.

"I don't know the steps," she protested, stumbling, as he held her hands up in the air.

"Just watch the dancers, you'll soon pick it up." He swung her round just as Ana and Hans took the floor. "See, if they can do it, you can."

Tessa relaxed, getting into the rhythm of the dance.

When the dance ended, everyone clapped for the dancers who had provided the demonstration.

Maria took them off to be fed in the kitchen.

The music changed to a slow dreamy waltz, and Tessa found herself gliding in Alex's arms.

As the music went on, Ana and Hans disappeared, to reappear later dressed in travelling clothes, waving goodbye. Everyone followed them out to where a car was waiting with Serge in the driving seat.

"Where are they going?" Tessa asked Alex.

"It's a secret," he whispered. "But I know Serge is taking them to the airport. Their bags are already in the boot."

Ana came back to Tessa, and kissed her on the cheek, "Thank you for all you've done for us," she said. "And you, Alex."

"Don't I get a kiss as well?" he said, leaning forward.

Ana pecked him on the cheek then slid into the car as Hans shook hands with Alex and followed her in.

Everyone waved and they were off.

"Bother," Tessa said. "I forgot the confetti."

"Never mind," Alex said significantly. "I'm sure there will be another occasion."

"So where did they go?" Tessa asked Serge as he came back from dropping Ana and Hans at the airport.

"I don't know." He grinned. "I just dropped them off. I expect they'll tell us when they get back." He went over to Maria, invited her to dance, and then spent the rest of the evening with her. It looked as if the party wouldn't end until the early hours.

Tessa and Serge were still staying with Alex at the chateau, so eventually Tessa, feeling tired, waved at Serge and was about to go up the stairs when Alex stopped her.

"I must get to bed," she said. "I've got to fix my flight back to England tomorrow. Now that Ana and Hans are reunited there's nothing to hold me here is there?" She looked into his eyes but couldn't read his expression. She hesitated, but Alex said nothing, turning away going back into the ballroom. She stared after him for a moment, then continued up the stairs to her room, gripping the banister hard, her thoughts in a whirl.

Next morning when Tessa came down to breakfast, she found Serge tucking into bacon and eggs, but there was no sign of Alex.

"He's been and gone," Serge told her, in answer to her unspoken question. "He said he had some urgent business."

Before Tessa could ask if he had left a message for her, Maria and Luka came in. Instead of sitting down, Luka came up to Tessa and stood by her shyly.

"Good morning Luka, good morning Maria," she said as

Luka scampered away to sit near Maria. Tessa noticed that Maria gave Serge a beaming smile as she passed.

"Are you going back to England?" Maria looked at Serge.

"Are you going, Tessa?" Serge asked.

"Yes, I must, but you don't have to. We've both got open tickets."

"I think I'd like to stay on for a bit." He smiled at Maria who blushed and fussed with Luka's chair.

Tessa smiled to herself.

After breakfast she phoned the airport and booked herself on to a flight that afternoon.

Why do I feel as if I'm running away? Or is it Alex who's running away from me?

She shook herself and went back to her room to pack.

Serge drove her to the airport, parked his car and helped her with her suitcase, waving goodbye as she went through the turnstile.

"I'll let you know when I'm coming back," he called.

"Thanks, Serge, see you soon."

A feeling of loneliness hit her as she walked to check in her suitcase. It had been quite an adventure, but now it was all over and she was on her way back home.

The feeling continued as she boarded the plane and sat in her numbered seat next to the window. Passengers were streaming on, struggling down the aisle with what looked to Tessa like larger cases that should have been checked into the baggage hold. She waited for someone to sit by her, but no-one came.

Bliss, an empty seat, I won't have to make conversation, I can just sit and dream.

As the plane taxied along the runway and took off, she looked at the empty seat next to her. *It should be Alex sitting next to me, but he didn't even see me off.* Tears came to her eyes as she looked at the mountains stretching out below her.

She took out her book and tried to read, but the pages

blurred before her eyes. She put the book away and settled down in her seat, closing her eyes.

Sometime into the flight she heard the familiar rattle of the trolley coming down the aisle. A male voice asked if she would like coffee and a sandwich. Opening her eyes and sitting up she said, "Just coffee, please."

She looked up, it was Alex.

He bent over her. "I can recommend the sandwiches," he said. "But if you don't want one, will you marry me?" He pushed the trolley away, urging her out of her seat as she melted into his arms. She felt a sense of relief and joy as their lips came together in a passionate embrace.

The air stewardesses were giggling in the background, and everyone on the plane applauded.

Embarrassed, Tessa slipped back into her seat, with Alex sliding in beside her.

"I'm sorry I couldn't see you before you left," he said, holding her hand. "There were a lot of loose ends I had to tidy up so that I could expand the firm's operations to England and live there with you. But you haven't said yes?"

Tessa turned to him, her eyes sparkling. "Yes, yes, a thousand times, yes."

He grasped her hands and drew her to him. "I've loved you from the moment we met. I want to be married to you, and I want to help you with your work on plastic waste. You've shown me how important it is."

Epilogue

Ana and Hans came over for Alex and Tessa's wedding, together with Maria and Serge, now engaged. Dr Faure would have liked to come but was too busy on a new project. He did, however, give Alex the rights to his flexible plastic as a wedding present.

Tessa and Alex got married in the small church in the parish near Tunbridge Wells, the service taken by Tessa's father. Practically the whole village turned up to see Tessa walk down the aisle in a flowing white dress. Serge acted as best man. Tessa's mother was overcome with tears of joy as her daughter and Alex stood in front of the altar.

Where did they go for their honeymoon? That's a secret that only they know, but undoubtedly it was somewhere warm with eternal sunlight. They came back, purchasing a house not quite as grand as Alex's Chateau but in the country within commuting distance of the University of Brookshire.

ABOUT THE AUTHOR

Pippa lives in the UK but has spent numerous summers in Montreal and PEI teaching university classes. Under different pen names she has published a series of books about a witch named Annabel who helps the people of her village, three books about a bear named Henry, numerous short stories in women's magazines, and many books on education. Canada and Crete are her favourite places. Hobbies include reading, walking and exploring.

Whispers in the Mind was her debut full-length romance novel, and she has followed this with *Love in the Lakes,* set in the English Lake District.

A Love of Dolls is her third novel, set in Switzerland.

www.ingramcontent.com/pod-product-compliance
Lightning Source LLC
Chambersburg PA
CBHW060819120626
46557CB00001B/284